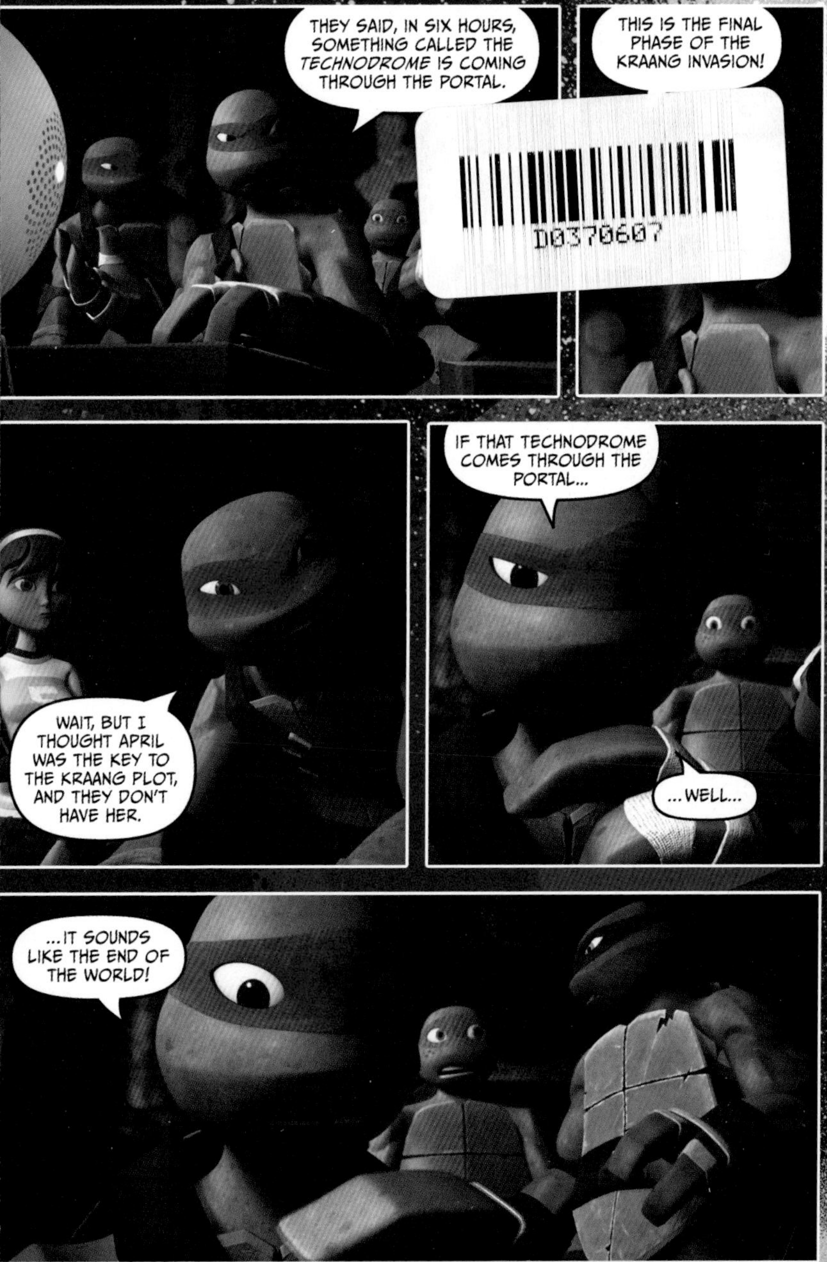
THEY SAID, IN SIX HOURS, SOMETHING CALLED THE *TECHNODROME* IS COMING THROUGH THE PORTAL.
THIS IS THE FINAL PHASE OF THE KRAANG INVASION!
WAIT, BUT I THOUGHT APRIL WAS THE KEY TO THE KRAANG PLOT, AND THEY DON'T HAVE HER.
IF THAT TECHNODROME COMES THROUGH THE PORTAL...
...WELL...
...IT SOUNDS LIKE THE END OF THE WORLD!

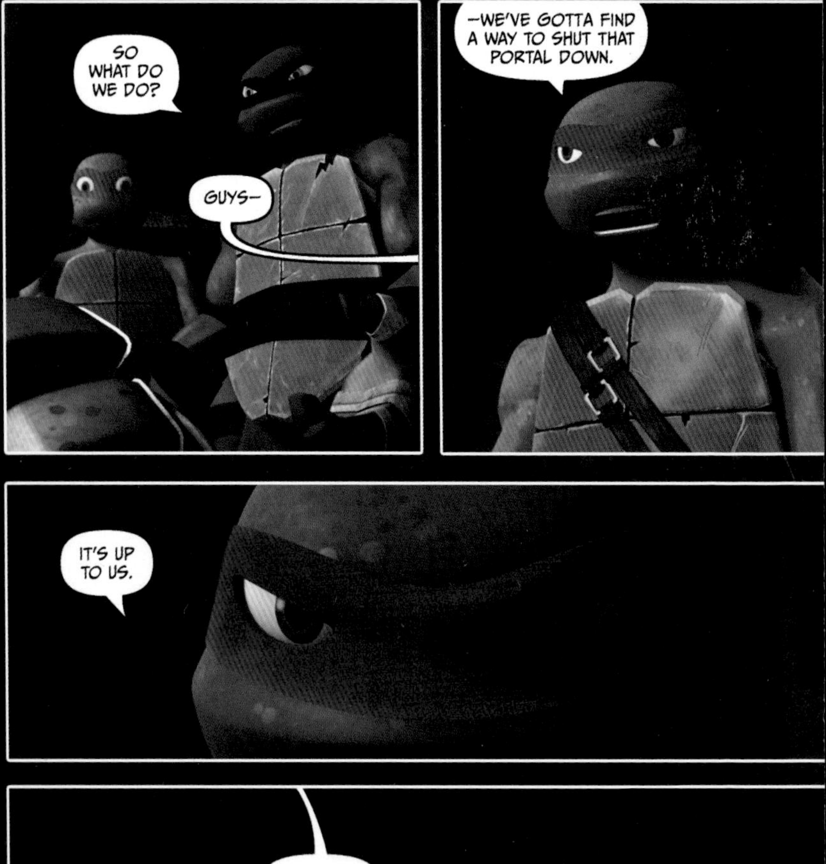
SO WHAT DO WE DO?
GUYS–
–WE'VE GOTTA FIND A WAY TO SHUT THAT PORTAL DOWN.
IT'S UP TO US.
LEONARDO IS RIGHT.

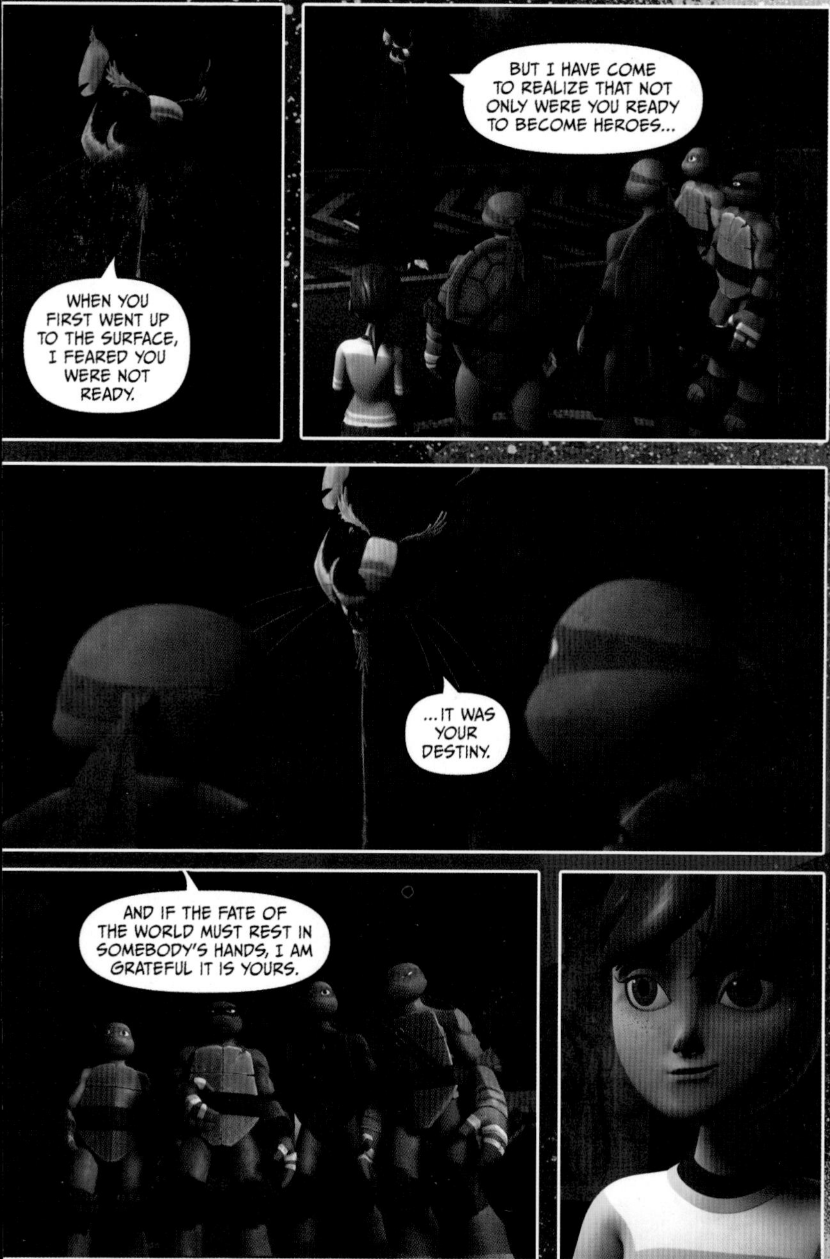
WHEN YOU FIRST WENT UP TO THE SURFACE, I FEARED YOU WERE NOT READY.
BUT I HAVE COME TO REALIZE THAT NOT ONLY WERE YOU READY TO BECOME HEROES...
...IT WAS YOUR DESTINY.
AND IF THE FATE OF THE WORLD MUST REST IN SOMEBODY'S HANDS, I AM GRATEFUL IT IS YOURS.

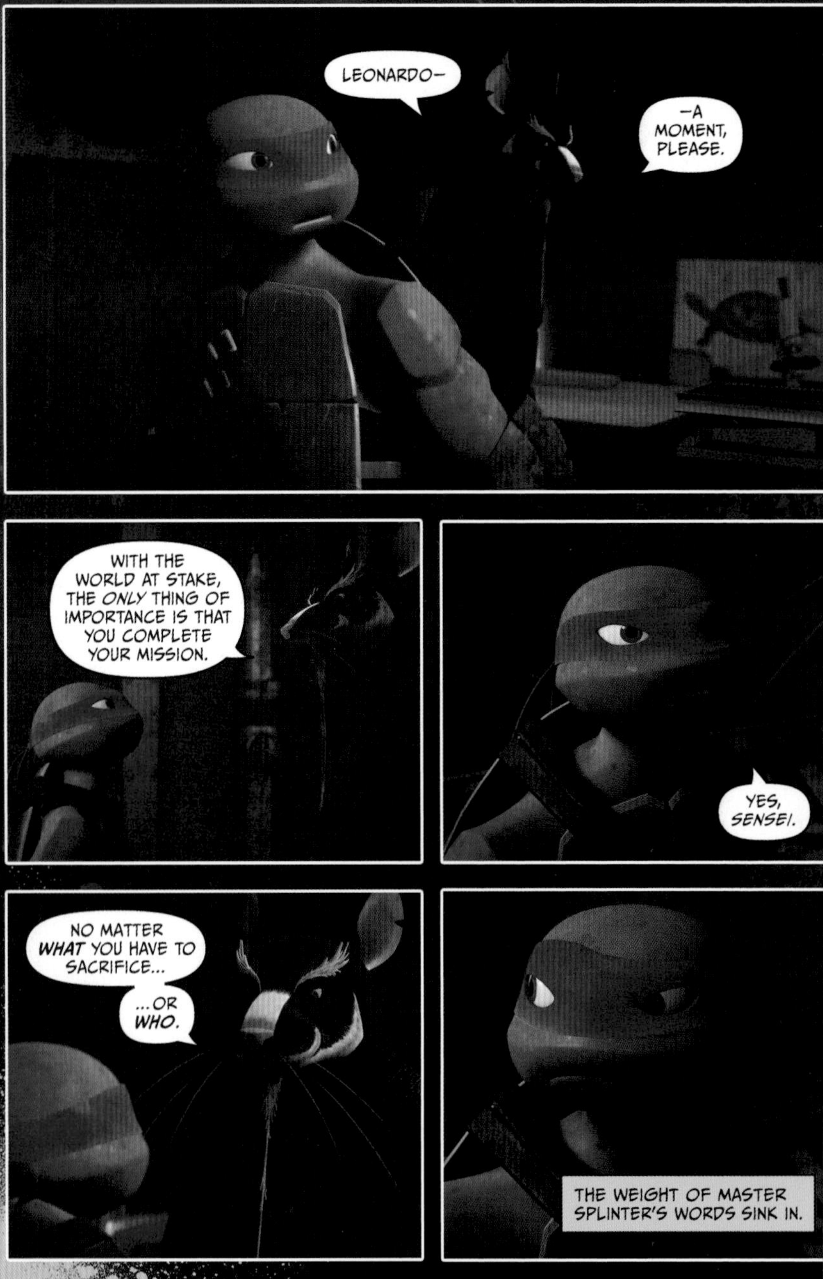
LEONARDO—
—A MOMENT, PLEASE.
WITH THE WORLD AT STAKE, THE *ONLY* THING OF IMPORTANCE IS THAT YOU COMPLETE YOUR MISSION.
YES, *SENSEI*.
NO MATTER ***WHAT*** YOU HAVE TO SACRIFICE...
...OR ***WHO***.
THE WEIGHT OF MASTER SPLINTER'S WORDS SINK IN.

WITHOUT DELAY, THE TURTLES PREPARE FOR THEIR MISSION.

DONNIE FIRES UP SOME HIGH-FLYING TECH...

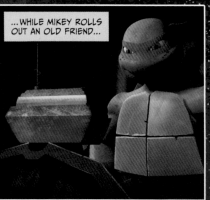

...WHILE MIKEY ROLLS OUT AN OLD FRIEND...

...METALHEAD!

SHING

AND AS RAPH ARMORS UP...

...LEO'S MASTER PLAN IS READY TO ROLL!

THE GROUP SAYS THEIR GOODBYES...

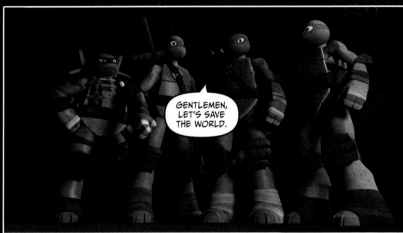

GENTLEMEN, LET'S SAVE THE WORLD.

SHELLRAISER

...AND THE SHELLRAISER TAKES OFF!

UM... SENSEI... DO YOU MIND IF I ASK YOU A QUESTION?

OF COURSE NOT.

WHY AREN'T YOU GOING WITH THEM?

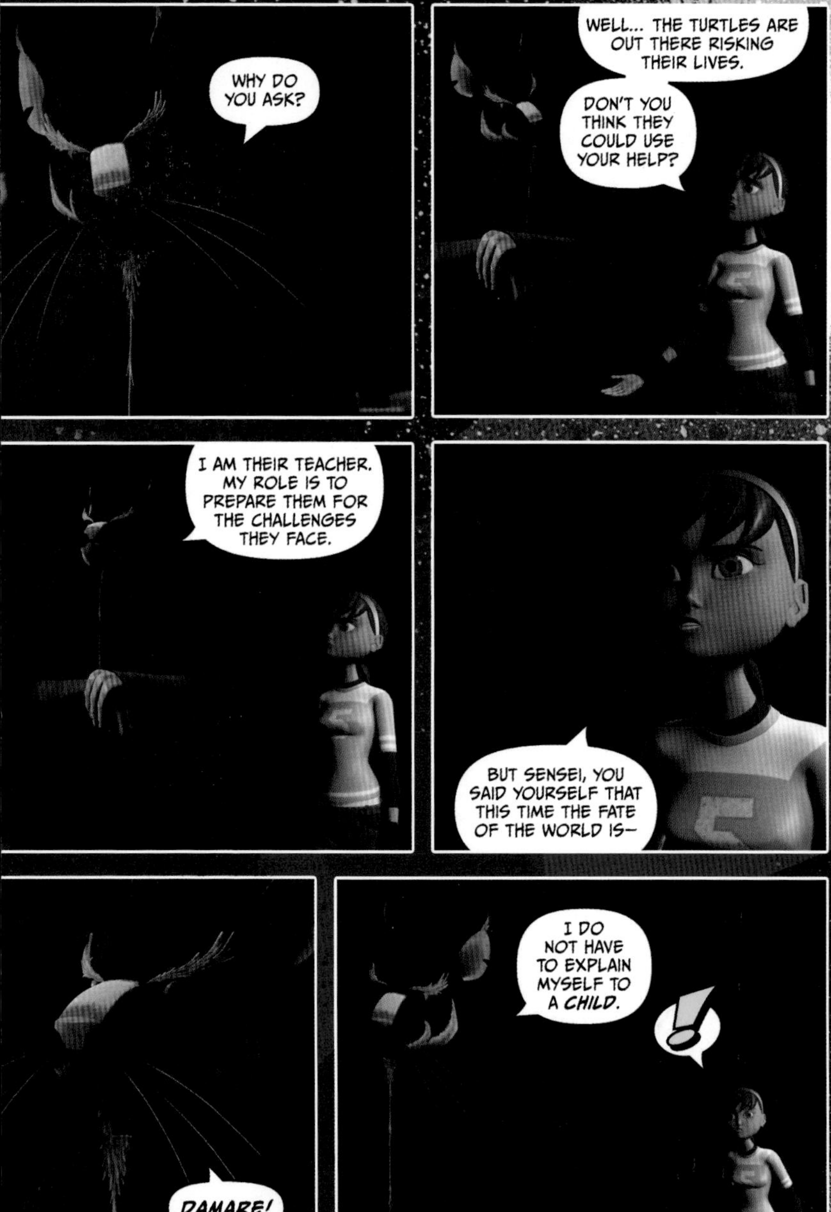
WHY DO YOU ASK?
WELL... THE TURTLES ARE OUT THERE RISKING THEIR LIVES.
DON'T YOU THINK THEY COULD USE YOUR HELP?
I AM THEIR TEACHER. MY ROLE IS TO PREPARE THEM FOR THE CHALLENGES THEY FACE.
BUT SENSEI, YOU SAID YOURSELF THAT THIS TIME THE FATE OF THE WORLD IS–
DAMARE!
I DO NOT HAVE TO EXPLAIN MYSELF TO A *CHILD*.
!

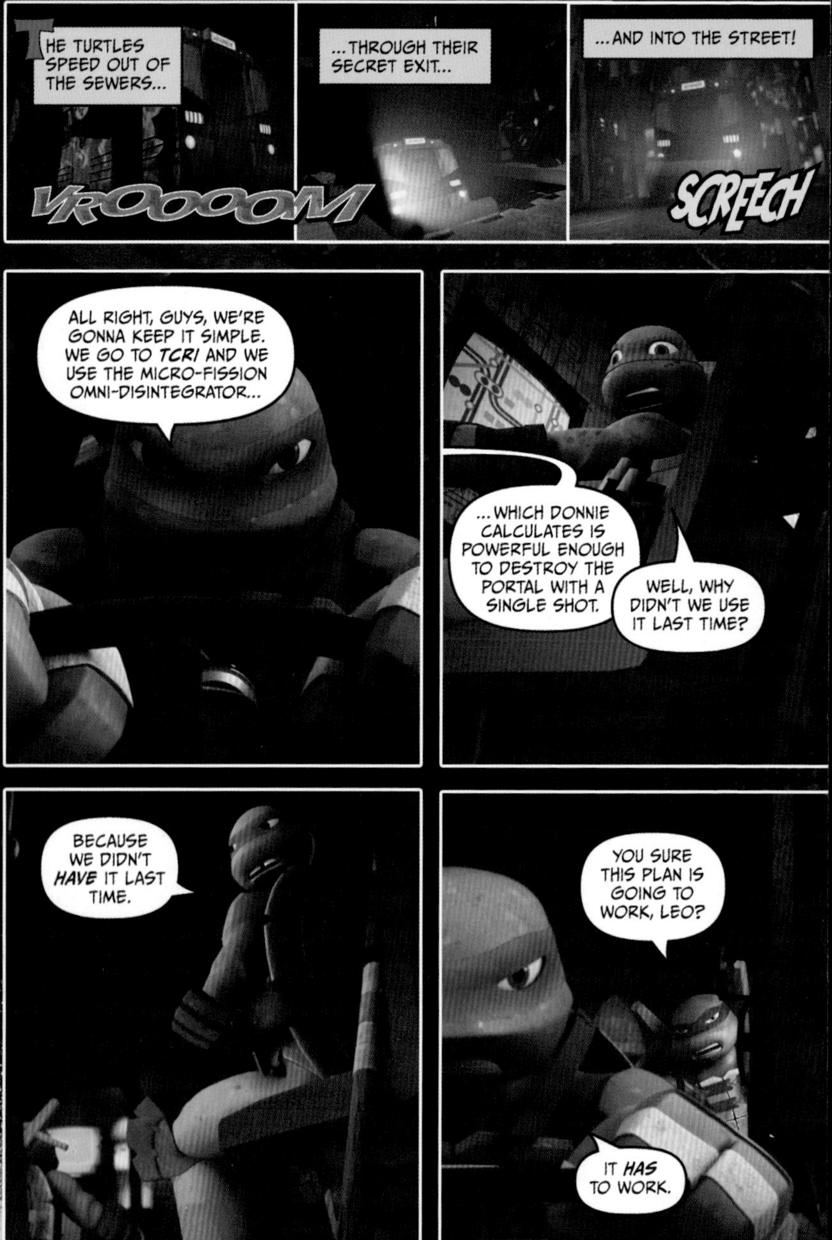
THE TURTLES SPEED OUT OF THE SEWERS...
VROOOOOM
...THROUGH THEIR SECRET EXIT...
...AND INTO THE STREET!
SCREECH
ALL RIGHT, GUYS, WE'RE GONNA KEEP IT SIMPLE. WE GO TO *TCRI* AND WE USE THE MICRO-FISSION OMNI-DISINTEGRATOR...
...WHICH DONNIE CALCULATES IS POWERFUL ENOUGH TO DESTROY THE PORTAL WITH A SINGLE SHOT.
WELL, WHY DIDN'T WE USE IT LAST TIME?
BECAUSE WE DIDN'T *HAVE* IT LAST TIME.
YOU SURE THIS PLAN IS GOING TO WORK, LEO?
IT *HAS* TO WORK.

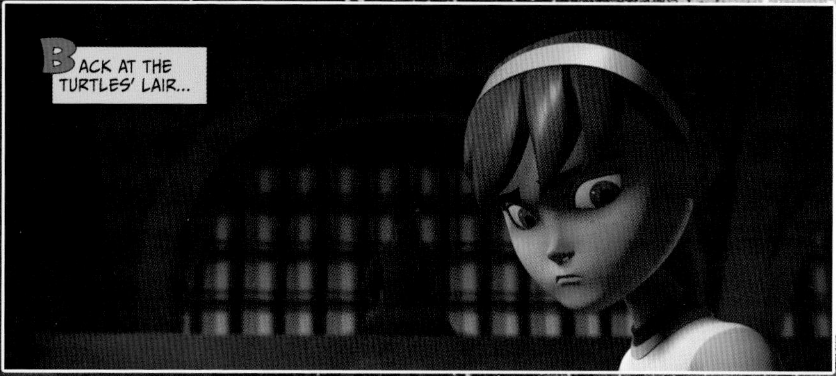
BACK AT THE TURTLES' LAIR...

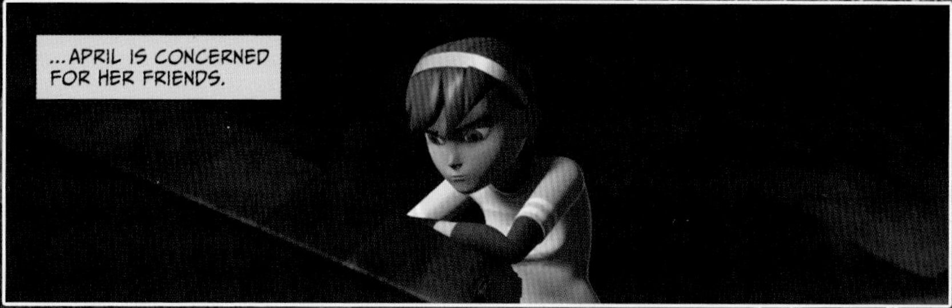
...APRIL IS CONCERNED FOR HER FRIENDS.

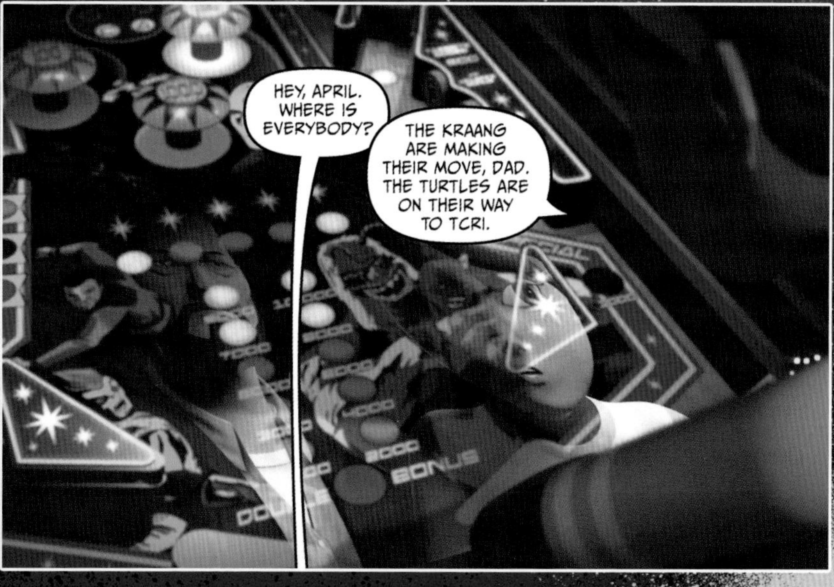
HEY, APRIL. WHERE IS EVERYBODY?
THE KRAANG ARE MAKING THEIR MOVE, DAD. THE TURTLES ARE ON THEIR WAY TO TCRI.
BONUS
DOUBLE

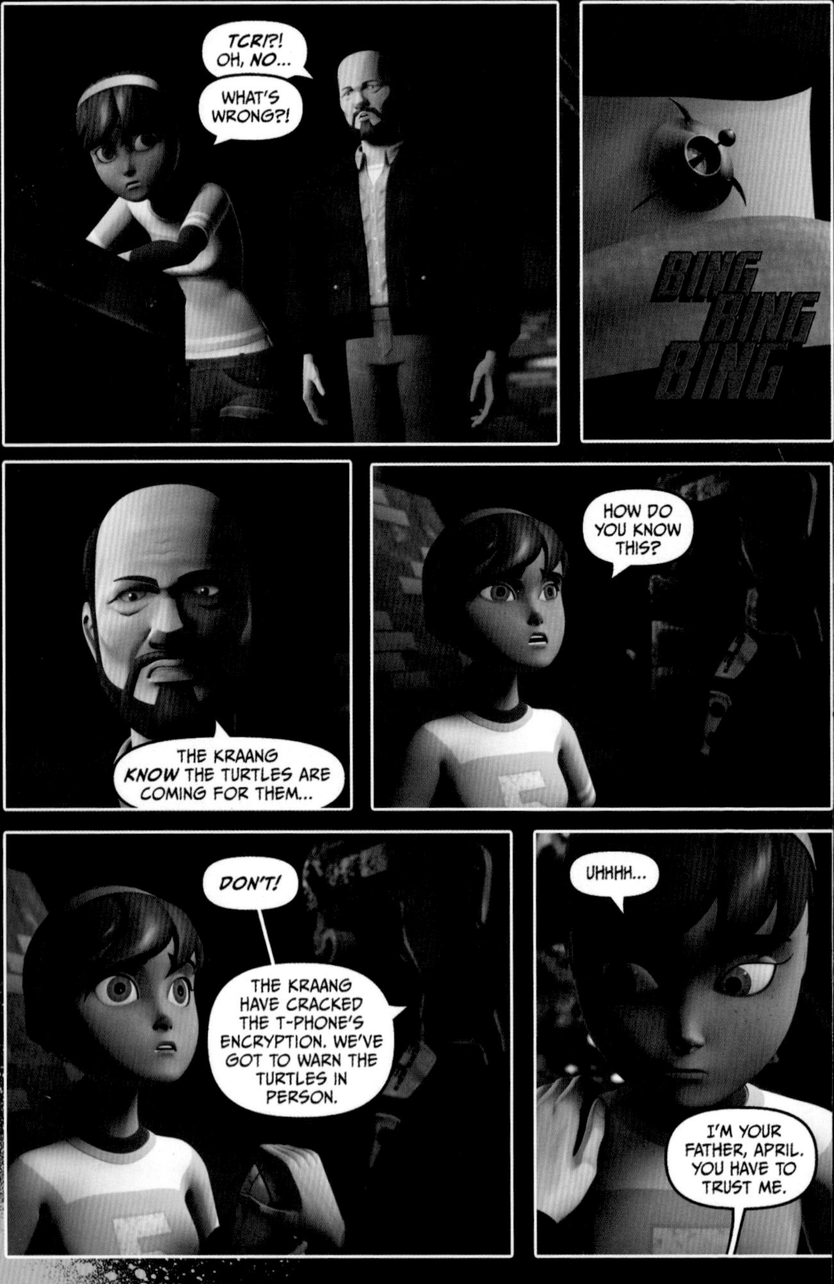
TCRI?! OH, NO...
WHAT'S WRONG?!
BING BING BING
THE KRAANG KNOW THE TURTLES ARE COMING FOR THEM...
HOW DO YOU KNOW THIS?
DON'T!
THE KRAANG HAVE CRACKED THE T-PHONE'S ENCRYPTION. WE'VE GOT TO WARN THE TURTLES IN PERSON.
UHHHH...
I'M YOUR FATHER, APRIL. YOU HAVE TO TRUST ME.

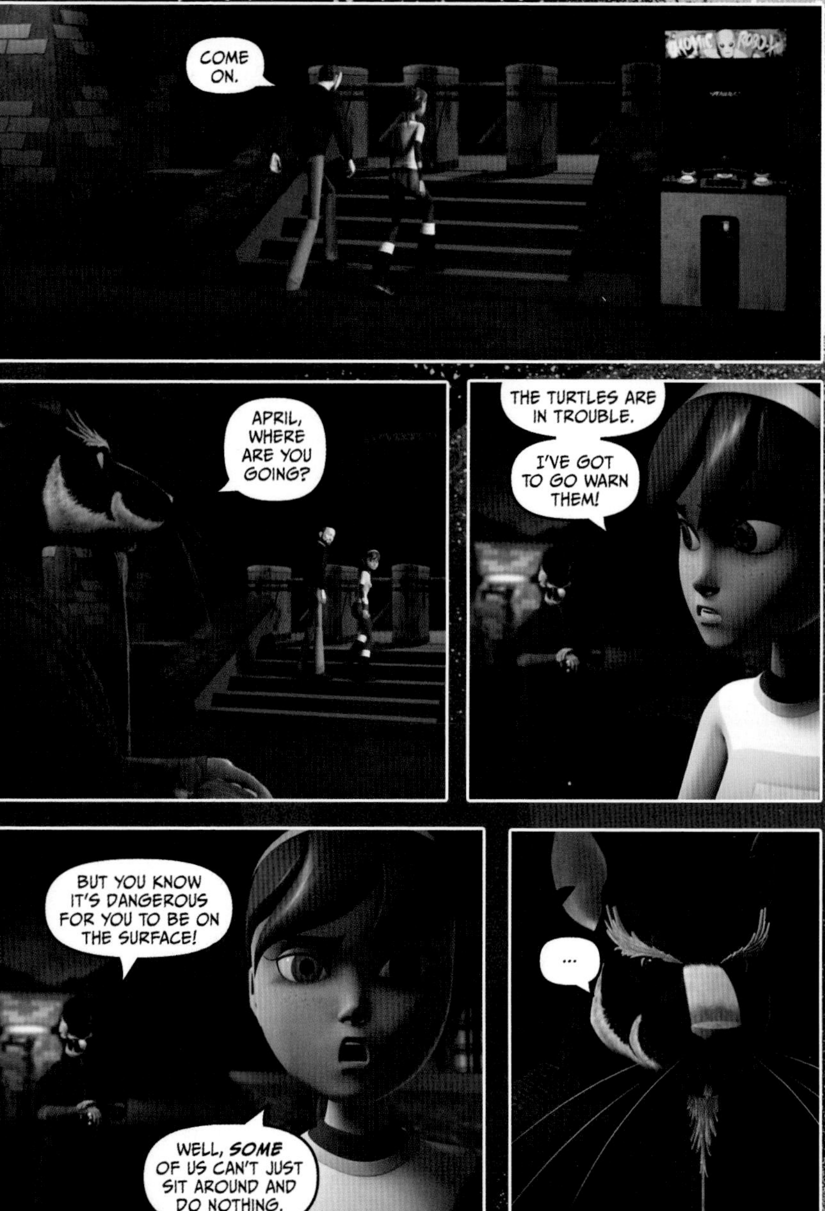
COME ON.
APRIL, WHERE ARE YOU GOING?
THE TURTLES ARE IN TROUBLE.
I'VE GOT TO GO WARN THEM!
BUT YOU KNOW IT'S DANGEROUS FOR YOU TO BE ON THE SURFACE!
WELL, *SOME* OF US CAN'T JUST SIT AROUND AND DO NOTHING.
...

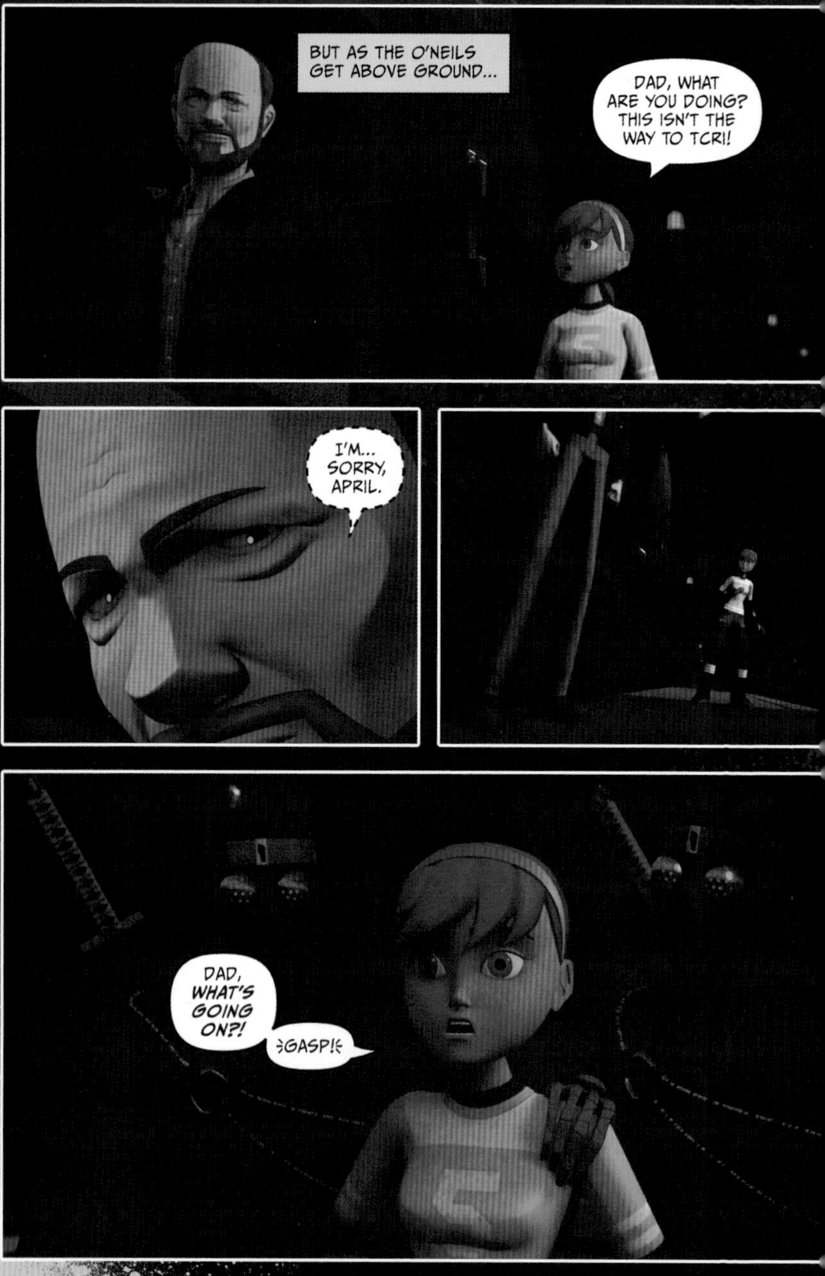
BUT AS THE O'NEILS GET ABOVE GROUND...
DAD, WHAT ARE YOU DOING? THIS ISN'T THE WAY TO TCRI!
I'M... SORRY, APRIL.
DAD, WHAT'S GOING ON?!
GASP!

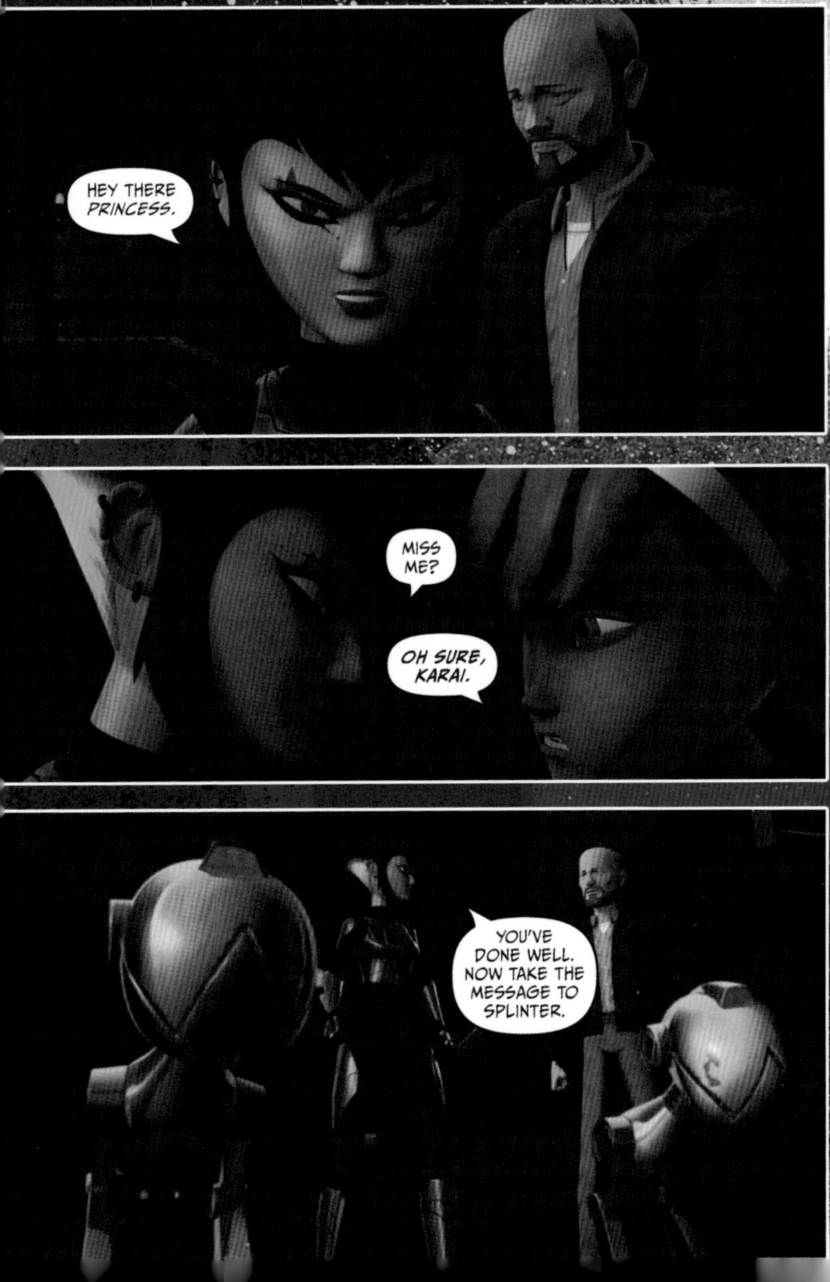
HEY THERE PRINCESS.
MISS ME?
OH SURE, KARAI.
YOU'VE DONE WELL. NOW TAKE THE MESSAGE TO SPLINTER.

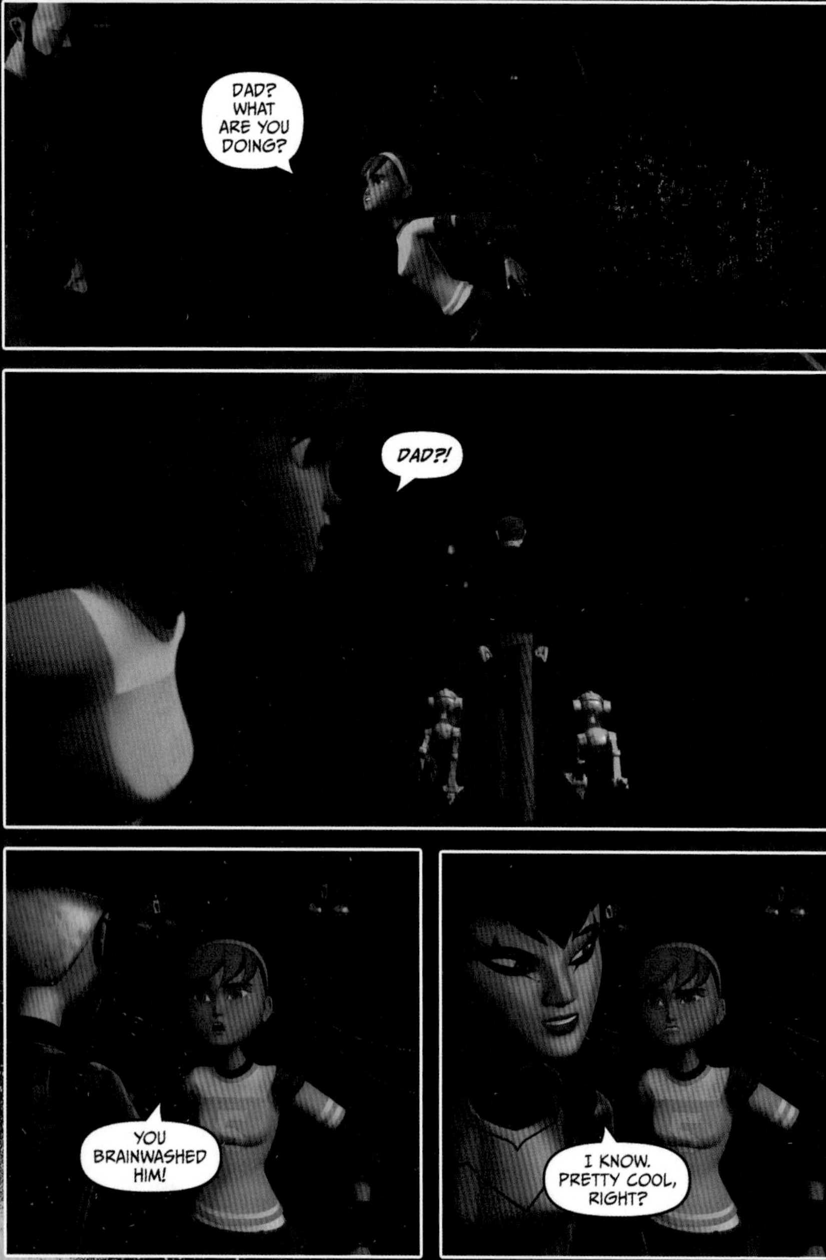
DAD? WHAT ARE YOU DOING?
DAD?!
YOU BRAINWASHED HIM!
I KNOW. PRETTY COOL, RIGHT?

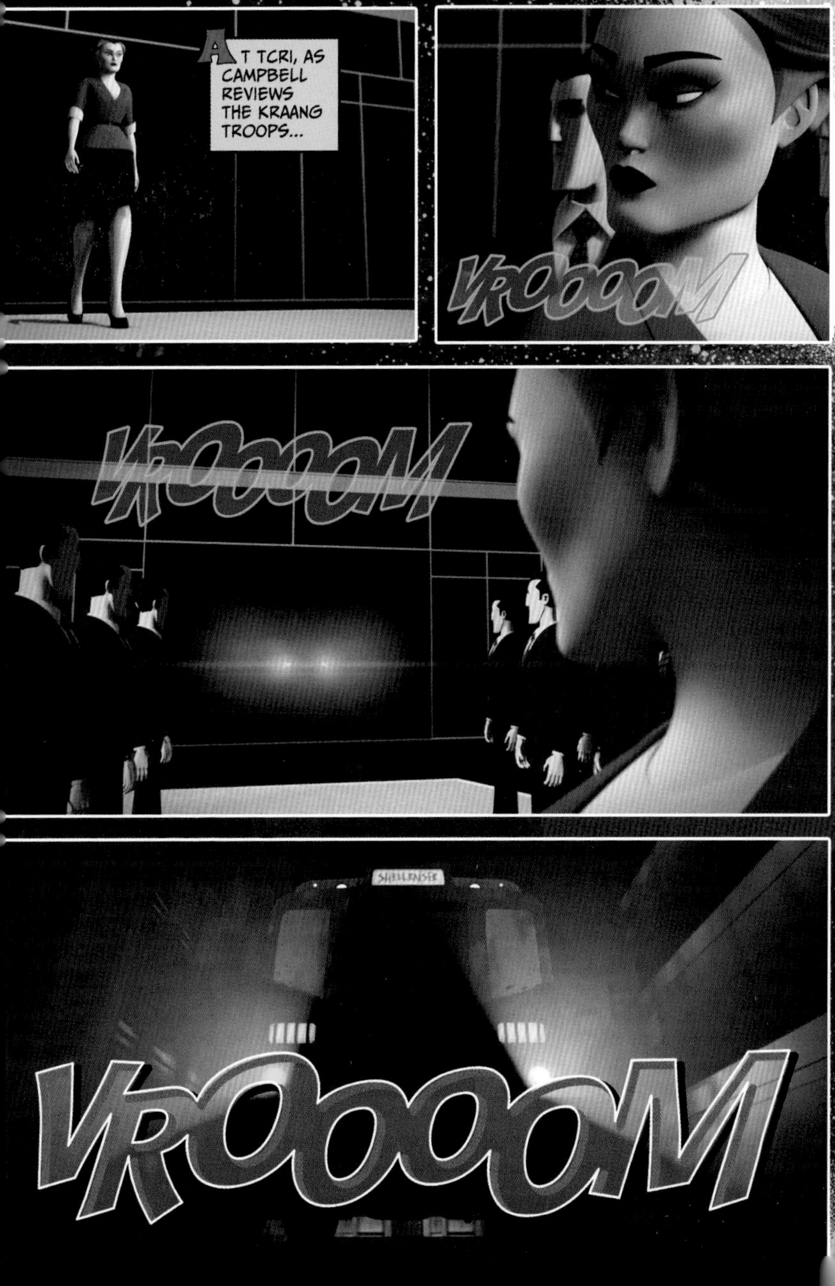
AT TCRI, AS CAMPBELL REVIEWS THE KRAANG TROOPS...
VROOOOM
VROOOOM
VROOOOM

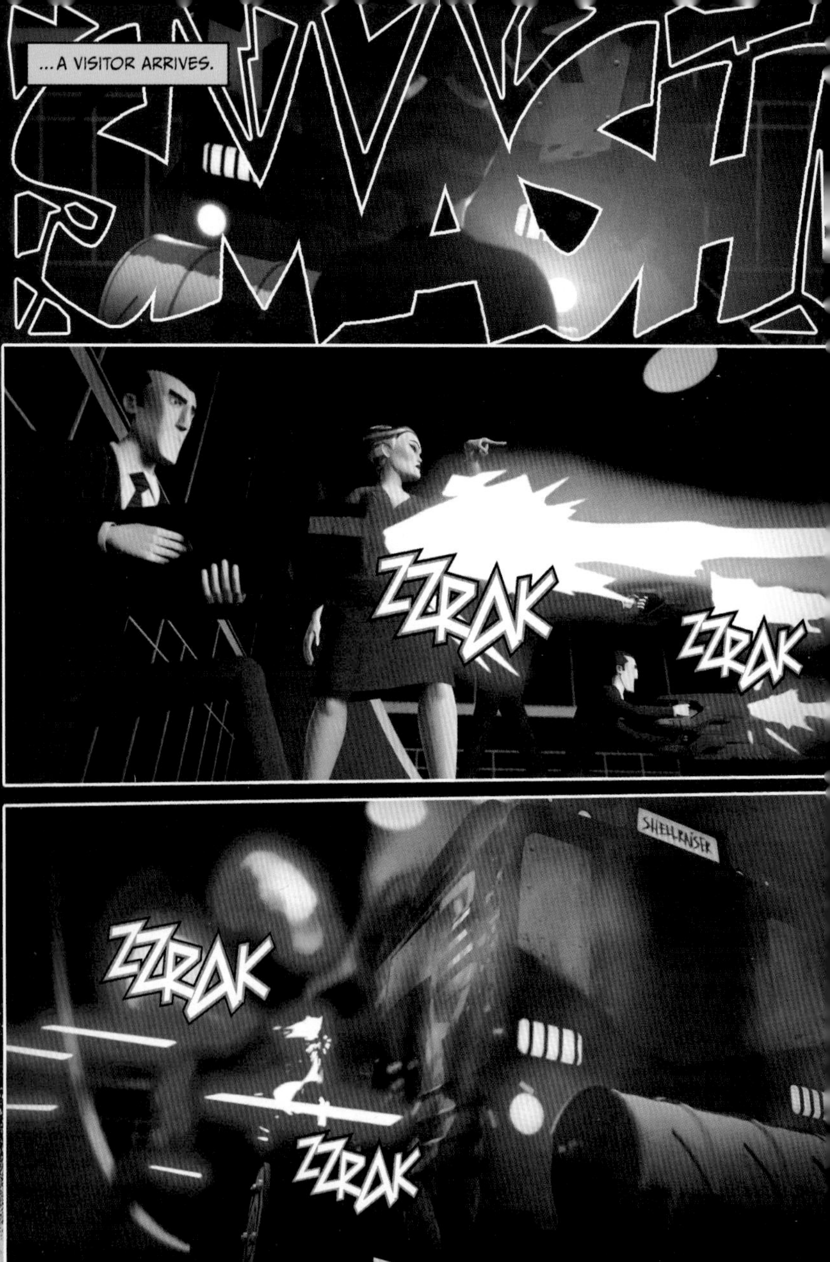
...A VISITOR ARRIVES.
SMASH
ZZRAK
ZZRAK
SHELLRAISER
ZZRAK
ZZRAK

ZZRAK ZZRAK ZZRAK ZZRAK

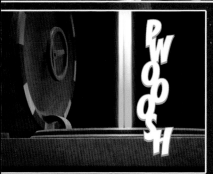

PWOOSH

BOOYAKASHA!!

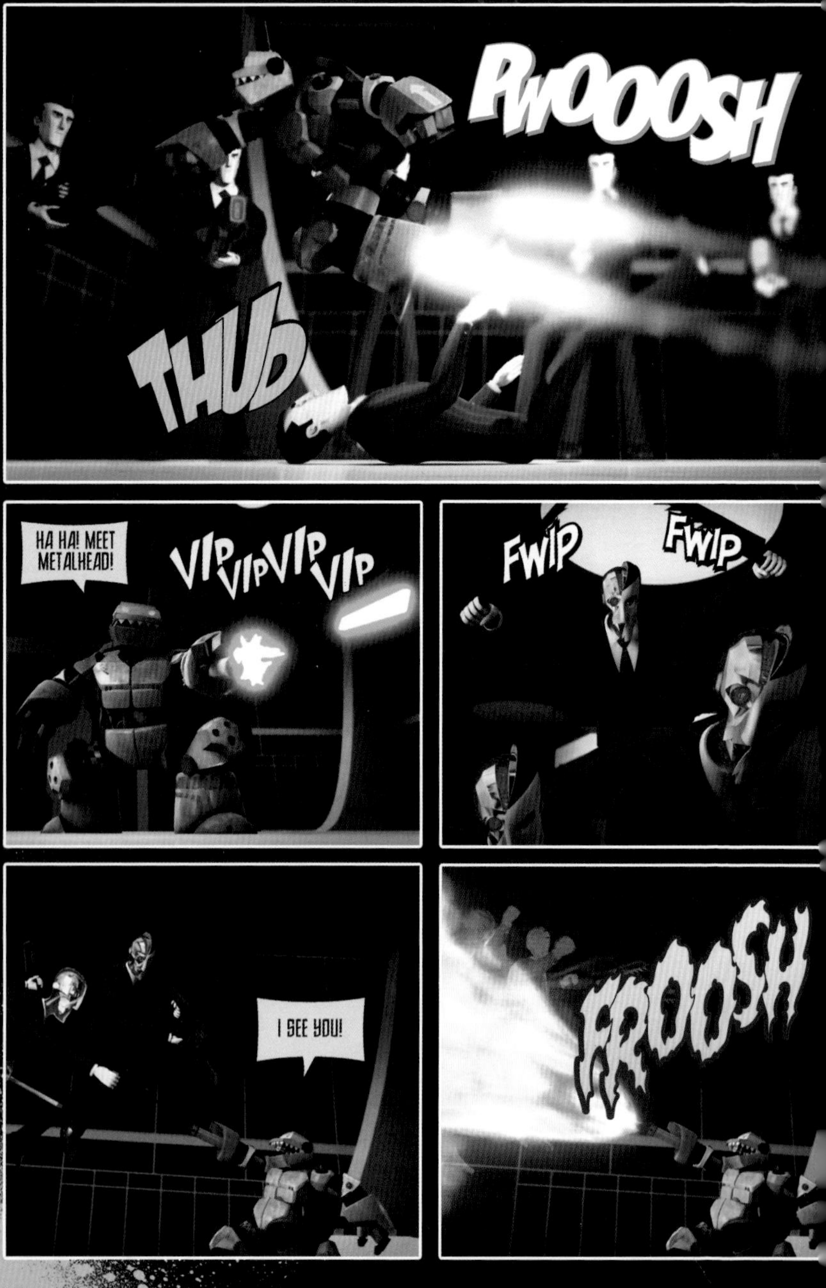
PWOOOSH
THUD
HA HA! MEET METALHEAD!
VIP VIP VIP VIP
FWIP
FWIP
I SEE YOU!
FROOSH

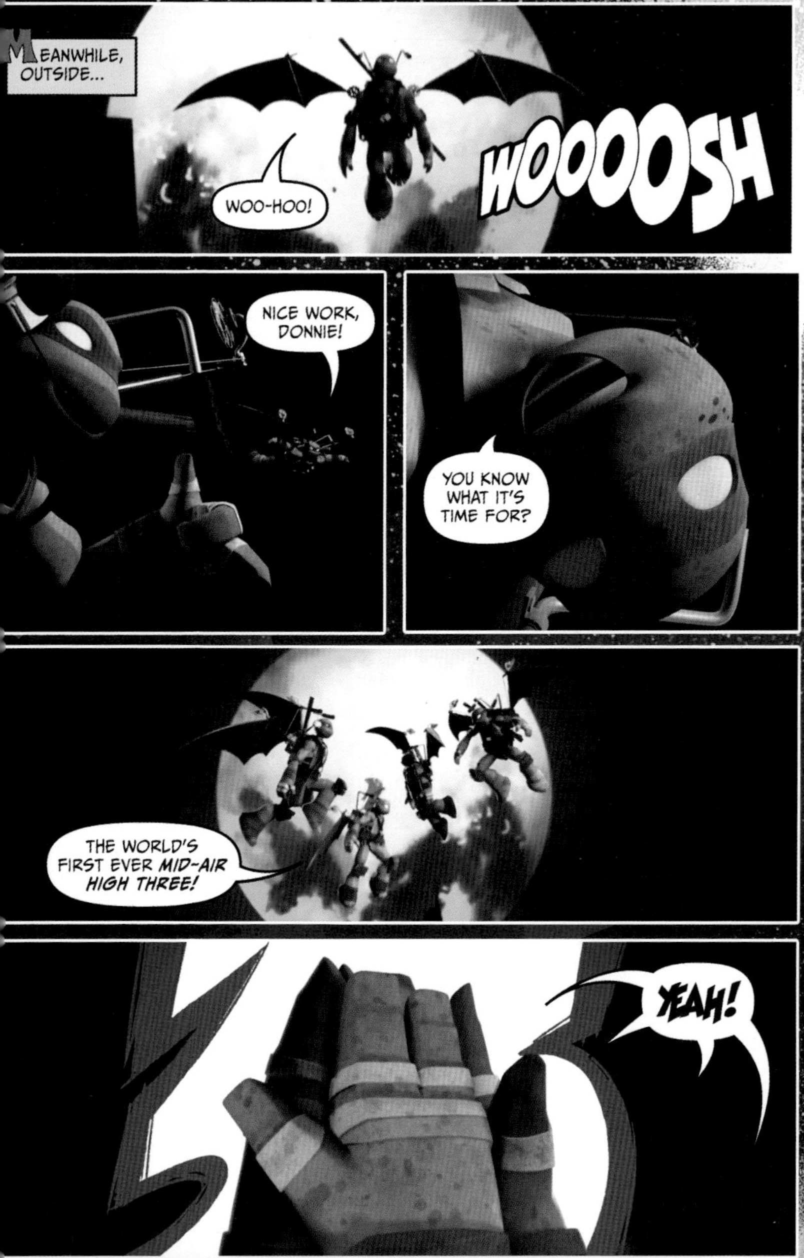
MEANWHILE, OUTSIDE...
WOO-HOO!
WOOOOSH
NICE WORK, DONNIE!
YOU KNOW WHAT IT'S TIME FOR?
THE WORLD'S FIRST EVER *MID-AIR HIGH THREE!*
YEAH!

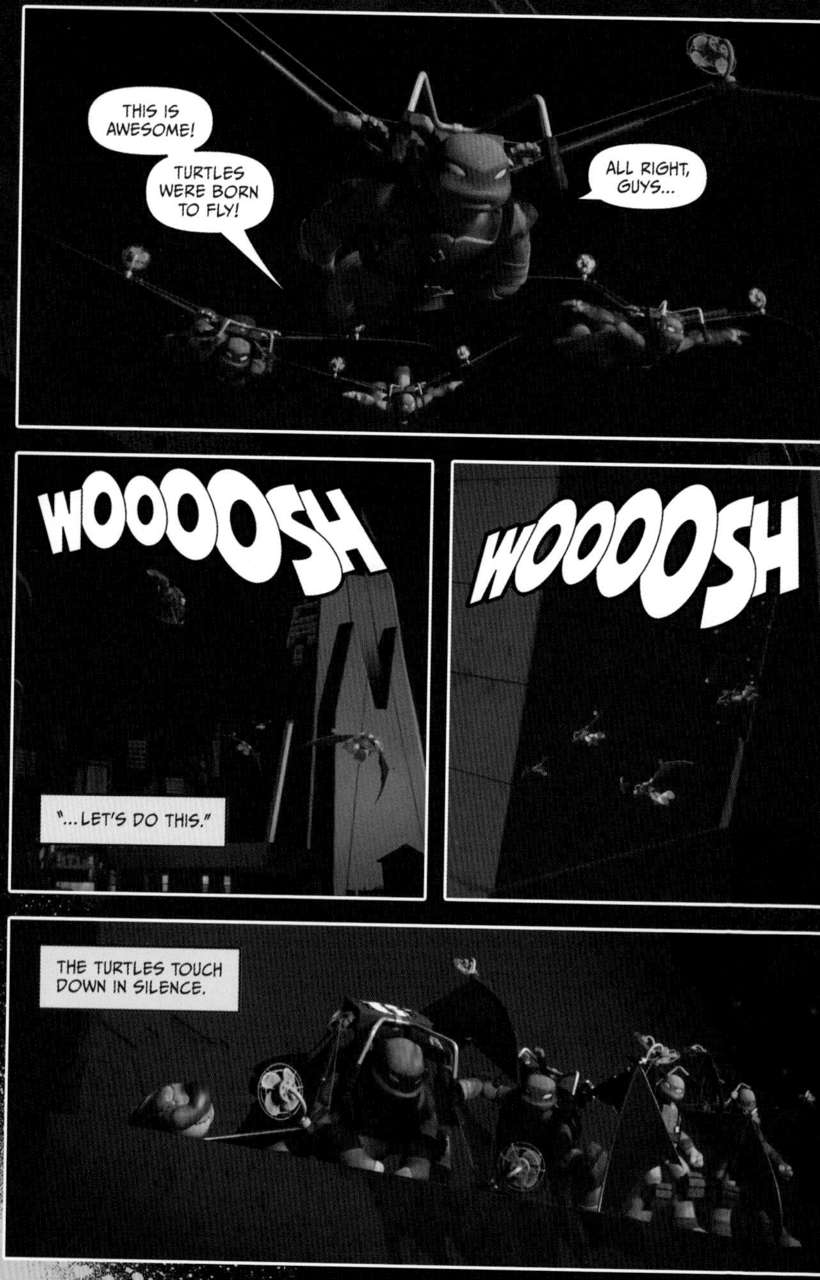
THIS IS AWESOME!
TURTLES WERE BORN TO FLY!
ALL RIGHT, GUYS...
WOOOOSH
"...LET'S DO THIS."
WOOOOSH
THE TURTLES TOUCH DOWN IN SILENCE.

WARBLE

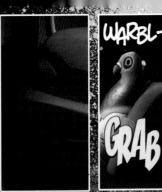

WARBL-

GRAB

INSIDE THE KRAANG COMPUTER ROOM...

WARBLE
WARBLE

?

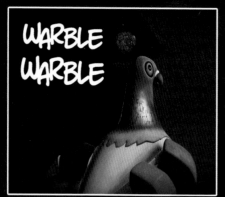

WARBLE
WARBLE

THANKS TO PIGEON POWER, THE TURTLES SNEAK PAST THE KRAANG SECURITY CAMERAS.

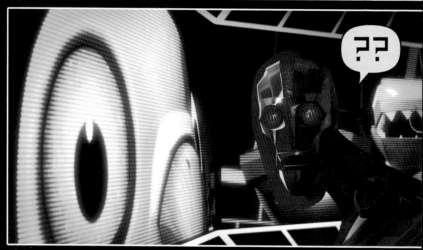

??

PAT PAT

SHHH.

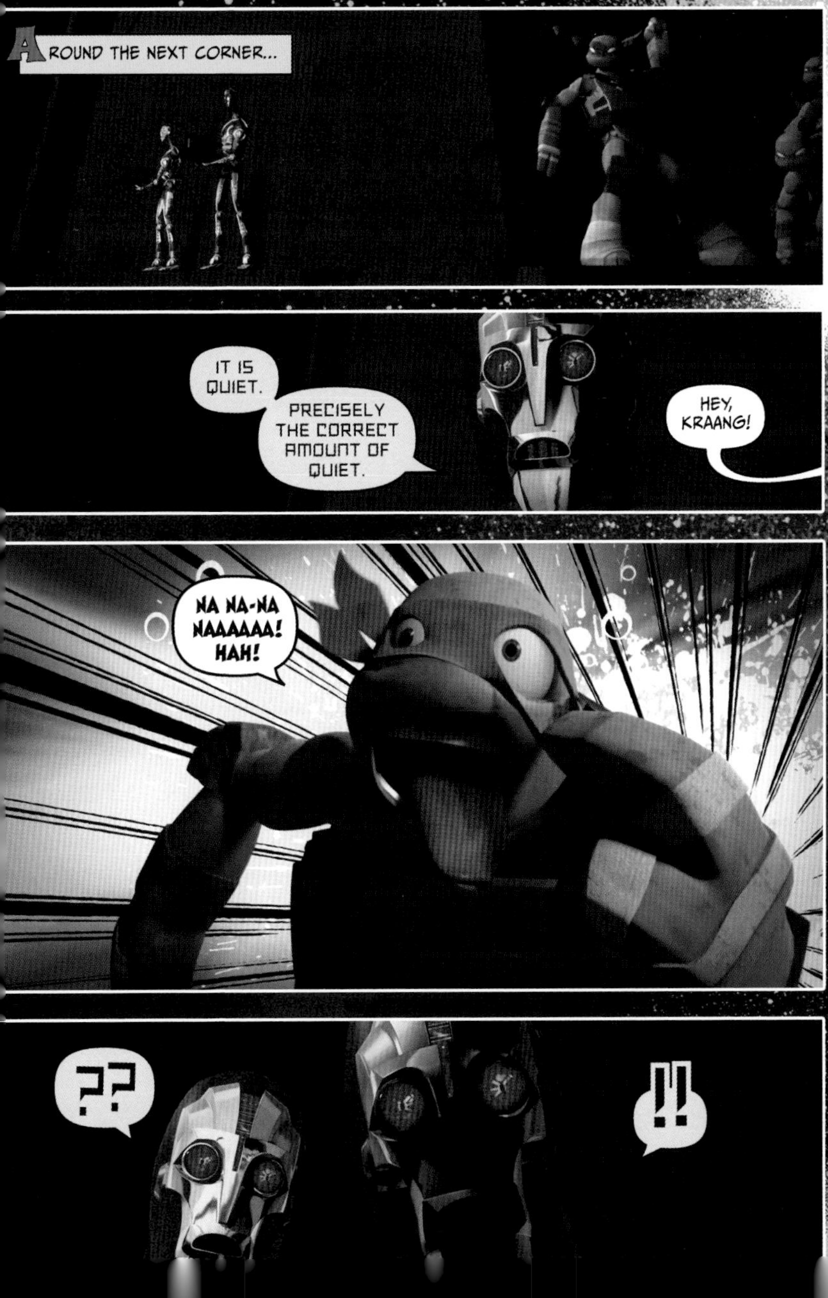
AROUND THE NEXT CORNER...
IT IS QUIET.
PRECISELY THE CORRECT AMOUNT OF QUIET.
HEY, KRAANG!
NA NA-NA NAAAAAA! HAH!
??
!!

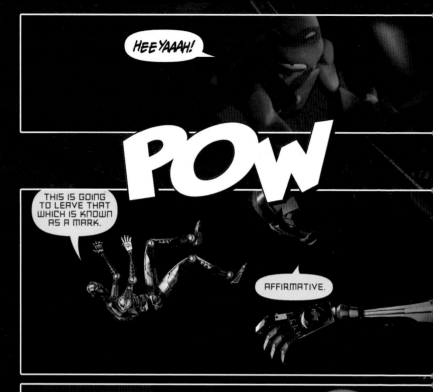

HEEYAAAH!

POW

THIS IS GOING TO LEAVE THAT WHICH IS KNOWN AS A MARK.

AFFIRMATIVE.

AND AS THE KRAANG GUARDS TAKE A SKY-DIVE...

...THE TURTLES MOVE ON IN.

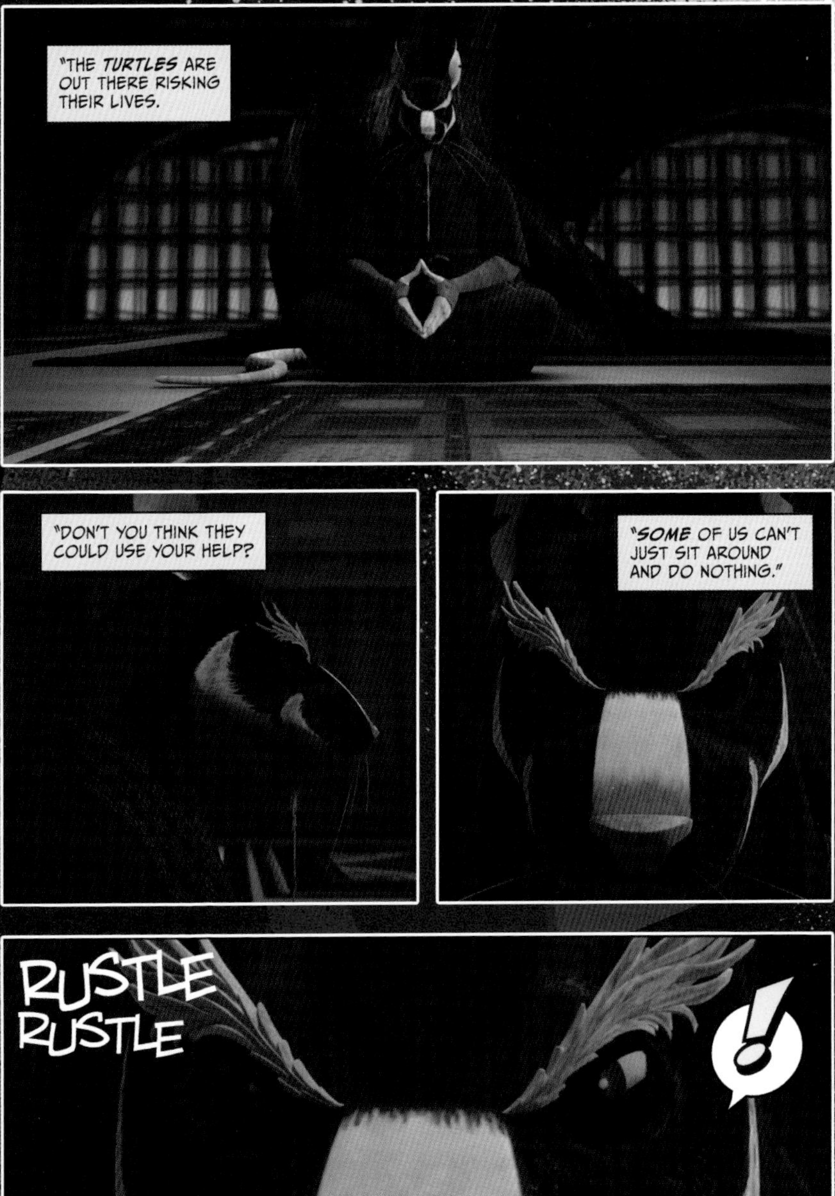
"THE *TURTLES* ARE OUT THERE RISKING THEIR LIVES.
"DON'T YOU THINK THEY COULD USE YOUR HELP?
"*SOME* OF US CAN'T JUST SIT AROUND AND DO NOTHING."
RUSTLE RUSTLE
!

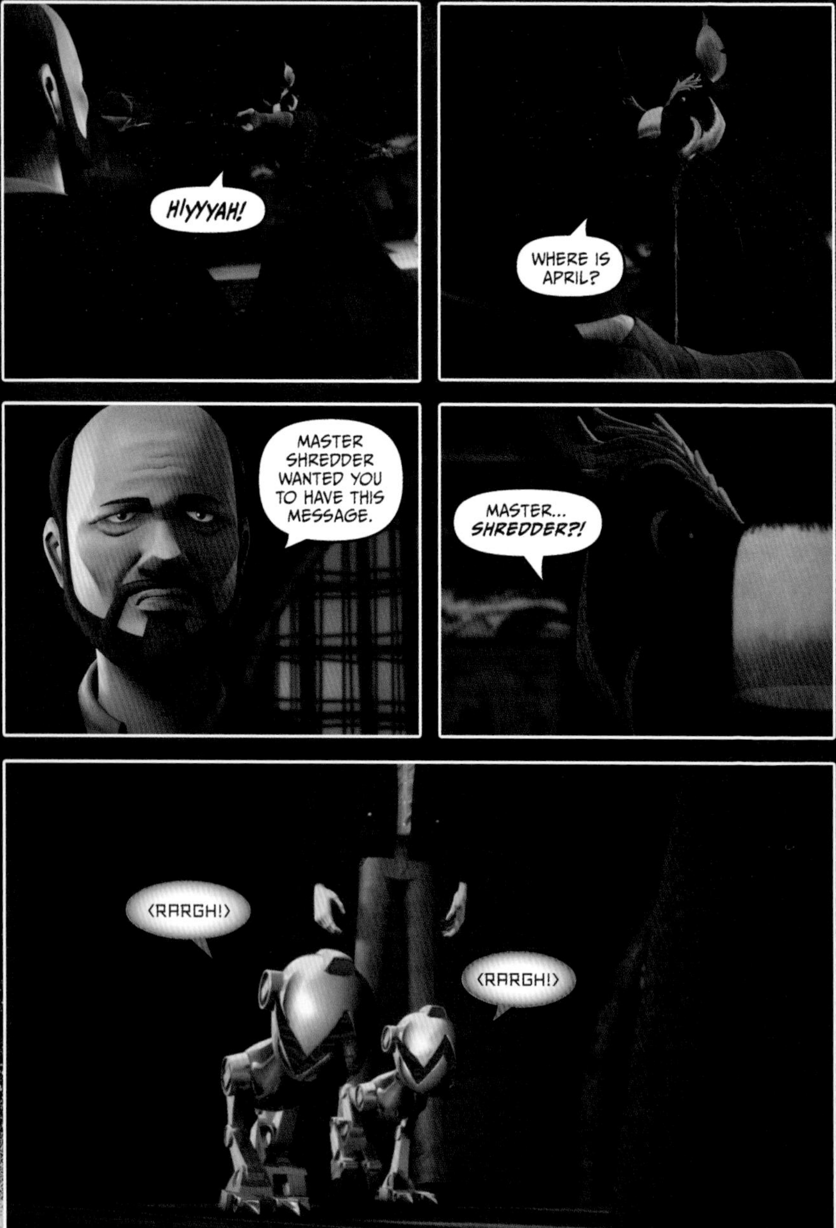
HIYYYAH!
WHERE IS APRIL?
MASTER SHREDDER WANTED YOU TO HAVE THIS MESSAGE.
MASTER... SHREDDER?!
<RARGH!>
<RARGH!>

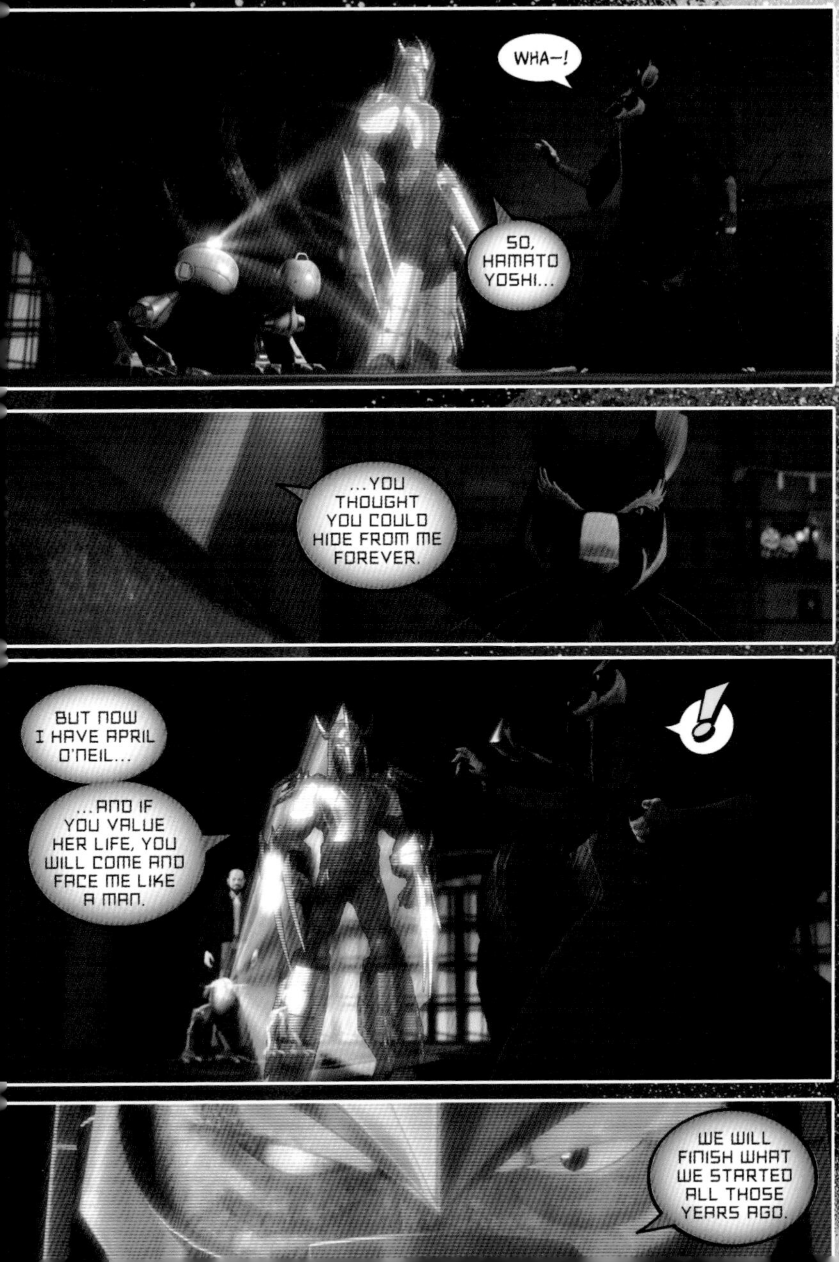
WHA—!
SO, HAMATO YOSHI...
...YOU THOUGHT YOU COULD HIDE FROM ME FOREVER.
BUT NOW I HAVE APRIL O'NEIL...
...AND IF YOU VALUE HER LIFE, YOU WILL COME AND FACE ME LIKE A MAN.
WE WILL FINISH WHAT WE STARTED ALL THOSE YEARS AGO.

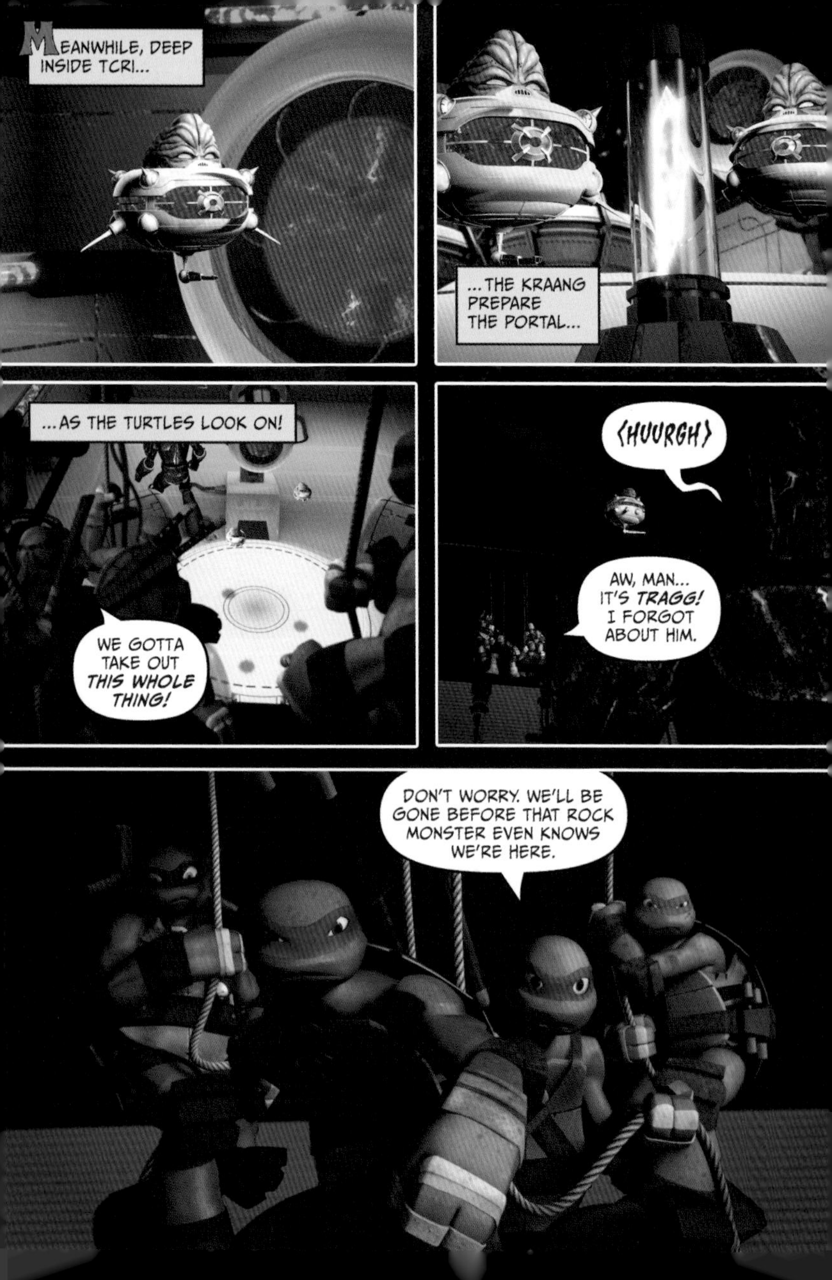
MEANWHILE, DEEP INSIDE TCRI...
...THE KRAANG PREPARE THE PORTAL...
...AS THE TURTLES LOOK ON!
WE GOTTA TAKE OUT THIS WHOLE THING!
⟨HUURGH⟩
AW, MAN... IT'S TRAGG! I FORGOT ABOUT HIM.
DON'T WORRY. WE'LL BE GONE BEFORE THAT ROCK MONSTER EVEN KNOWS WE'RE HERE.

OKAY, GUYS.

LEO READIES THE MICRO-FISSION OMNI-DISINTEGRATOR.

THIS ALL ENDS IN...

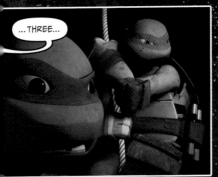

...THREE...

...TWO...

...ONE.

BOOOSH

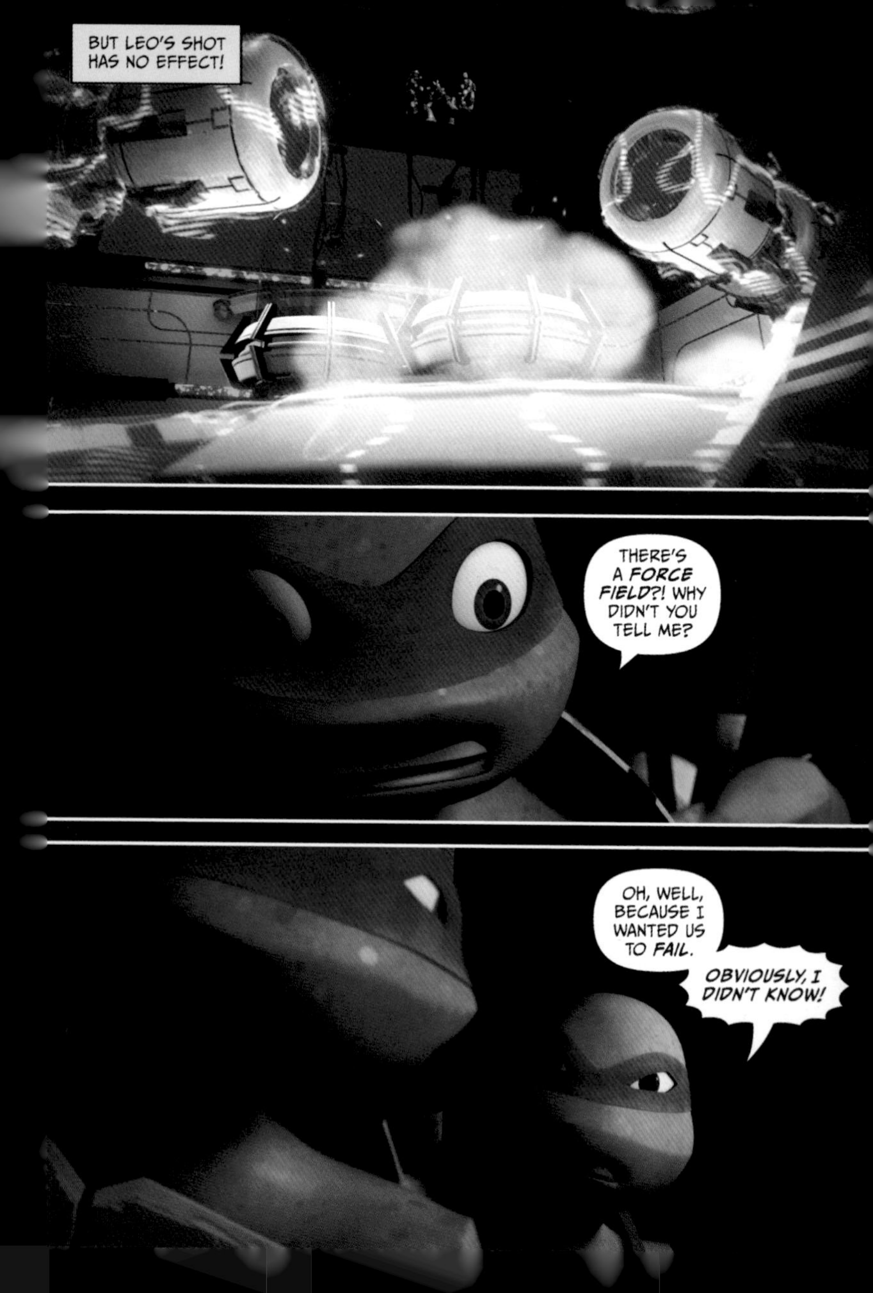
BUT LEO'S SHOT HAS NO EFFECT!
THERE'S A *FORCE FIELD?!* WHY DIDN'T YOU TELL ME?
OH, WELL, BECAUSE I WANTED US TO *FAIL*.
OBVIOUSLY, I DIDN'T KNOW!

UHHH...

...ANYONE GOT A *PLAN B?*

〈RAAARRG〉

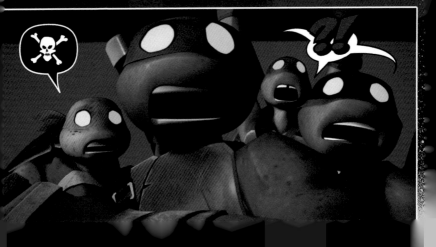

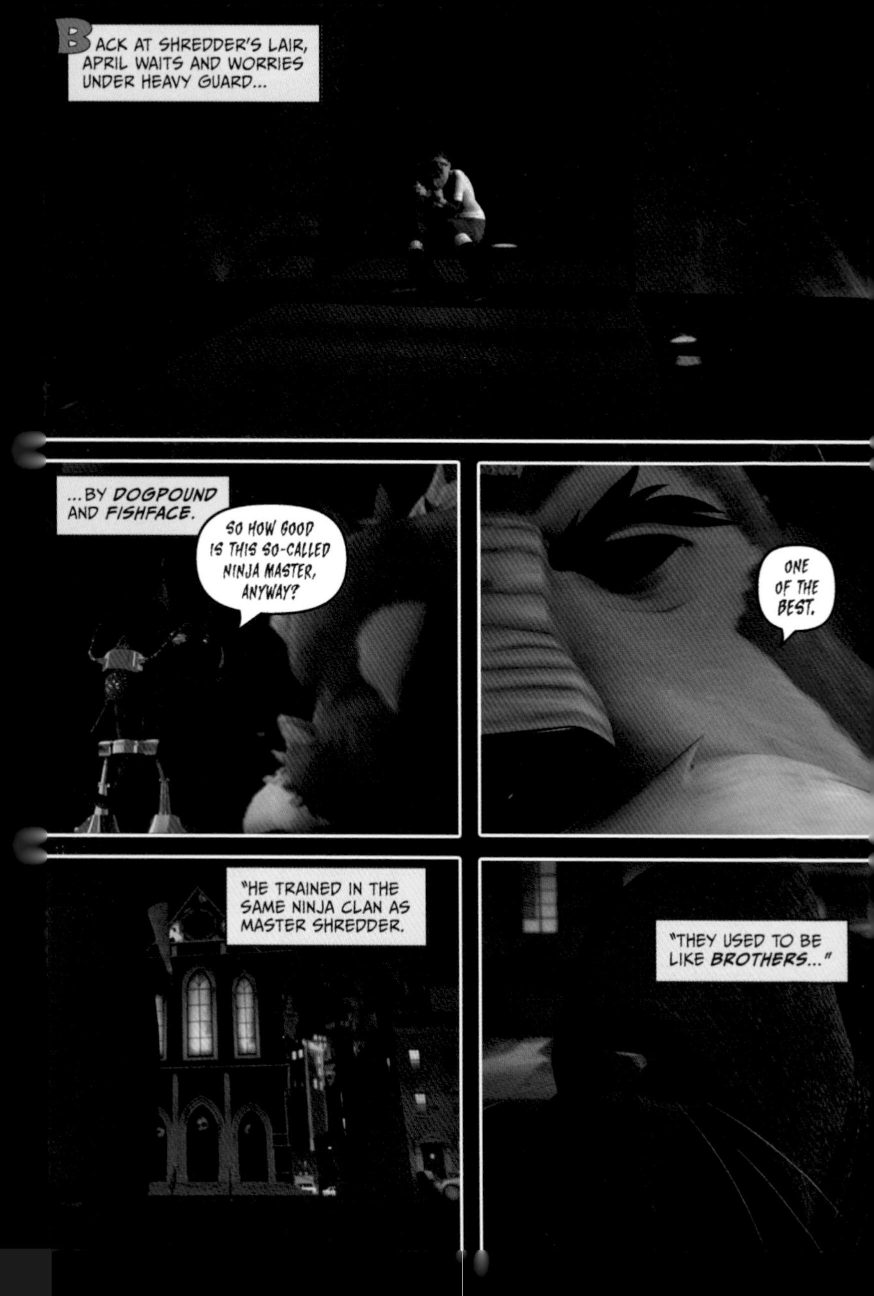
BACK AT SHREDDER'S LAIR, APRIL WAITS AND WORRIES UNDER HEAVY GUARD...
...BY DOGPOUND AND FISHFACE.
SO HOW GOOD IS THIS SO-CALLED NINJA MASTER, ANYWAY?
ONE OF THE BEST.
"HE TRAINED IN THE SAME NINJA CLAN AS MASTER SHREDDER.
"THEY USED TO BE LIKE BROTHERS..."

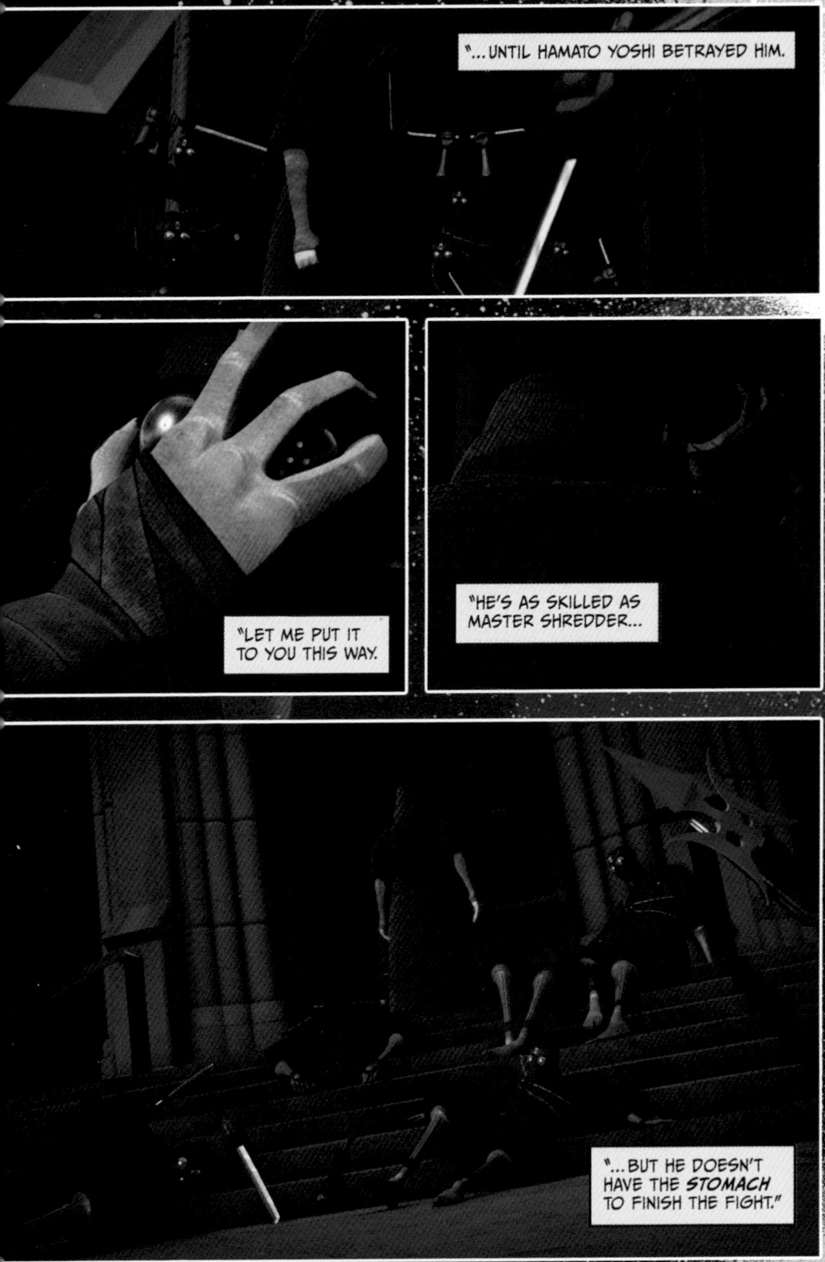
"...UNTIL HAMATO YOSHI BETRAYED HIM.
"LET ME PUT IT TO YOU THIS WAY.
"HE'S AS SKILLED AS MASTER SHREDDER...
"...BUT HE DOESN'T HAVE THE STOMACH TO FINISH THE FIGHT."

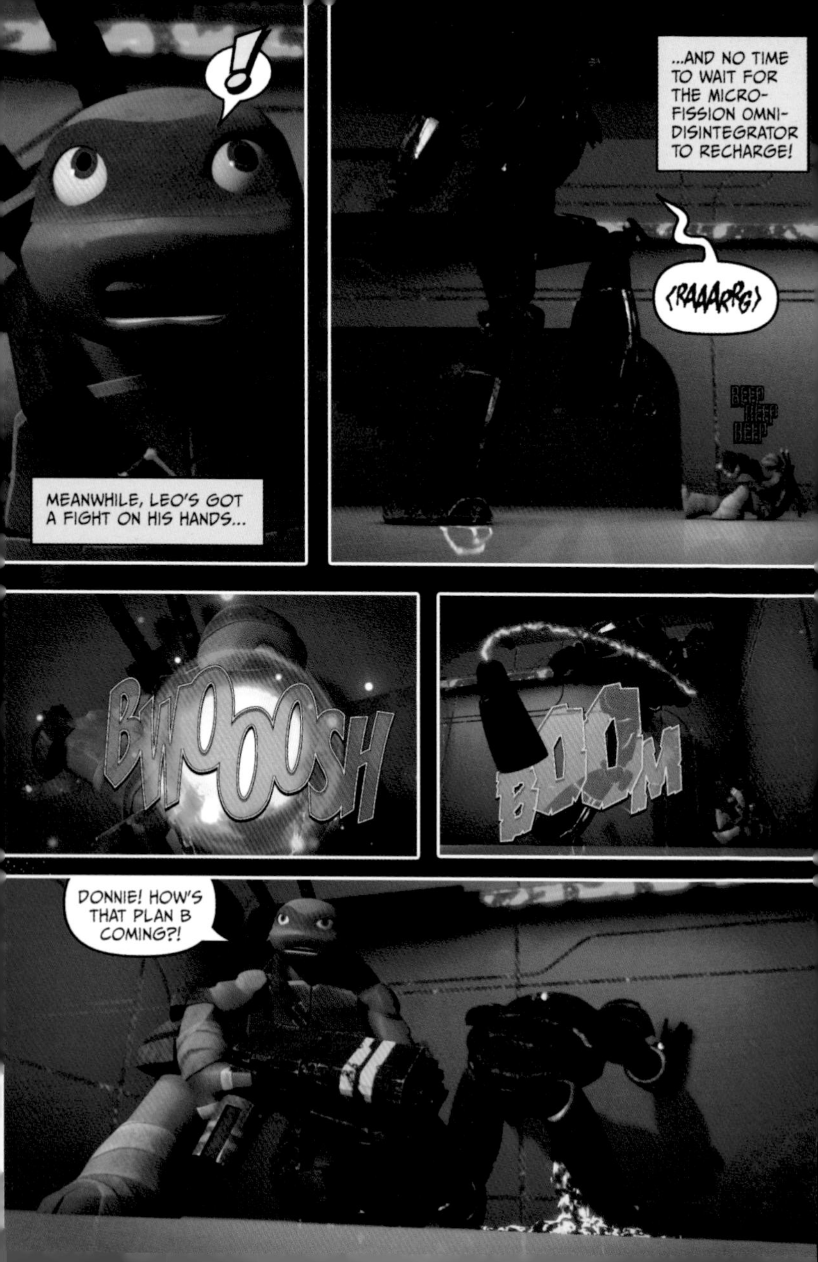
!
MEANWHILE, LEO'S GOT A FIGHT ON HIS HANDS...
...AND NO TIME TO WAIT FOR THE MICRO-FISSION OMNI-DISINTEGRATOR TO RECHARGE!
<RAAARRG>
BEEP BEEP BEEP
BWOOOSH
BOOM
DONNIE! HOW'S THAT PLAN B COMING?!

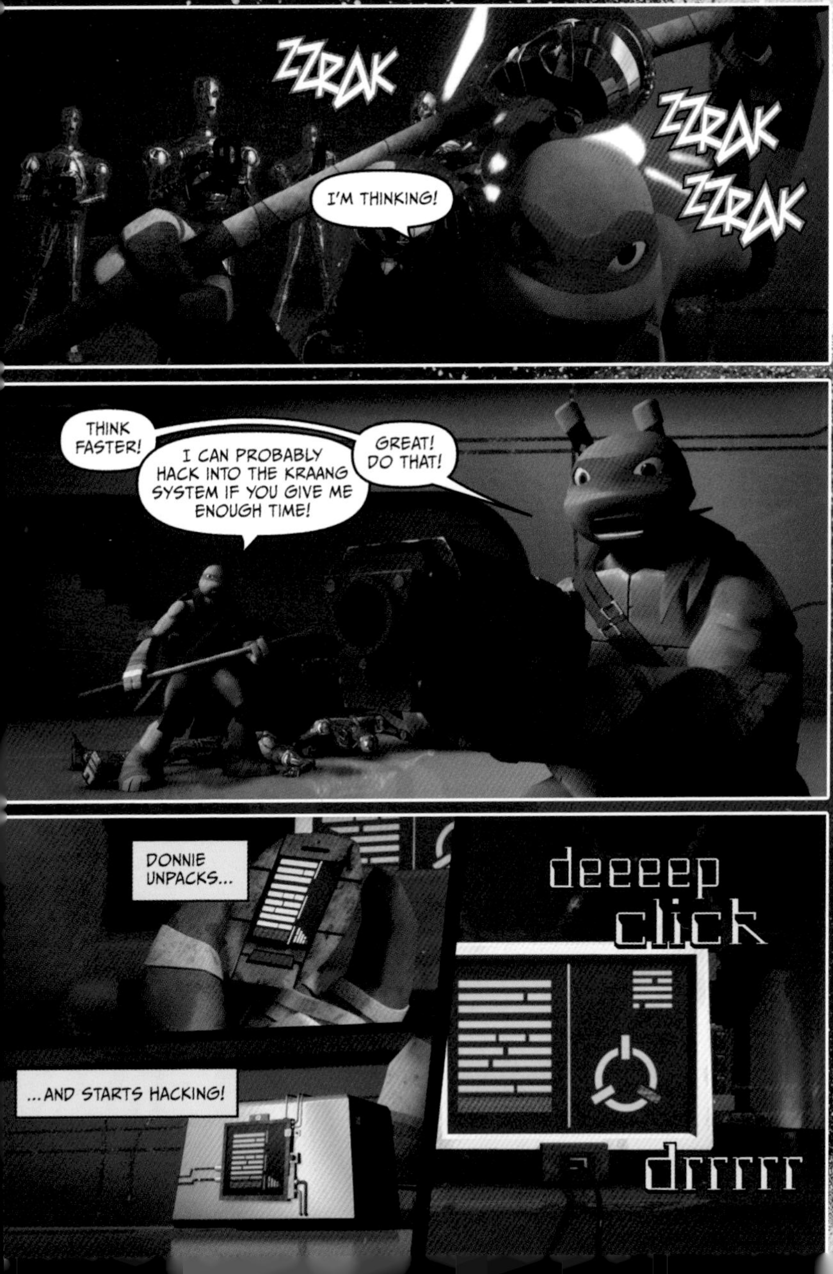
ZZRAK
ZZRAK
ZZRAK
I'M THINKING!
THINK FASTER!
I CAN PROBABLY HACK INTO THE KRAANG SYSTEM IF YOU GIVE ME ENOUGH TIME!
GREAT! DO THAT!
DONNIE UNPACKS...
deeeep
click
...AND STARTS HACKING!
drrrrr

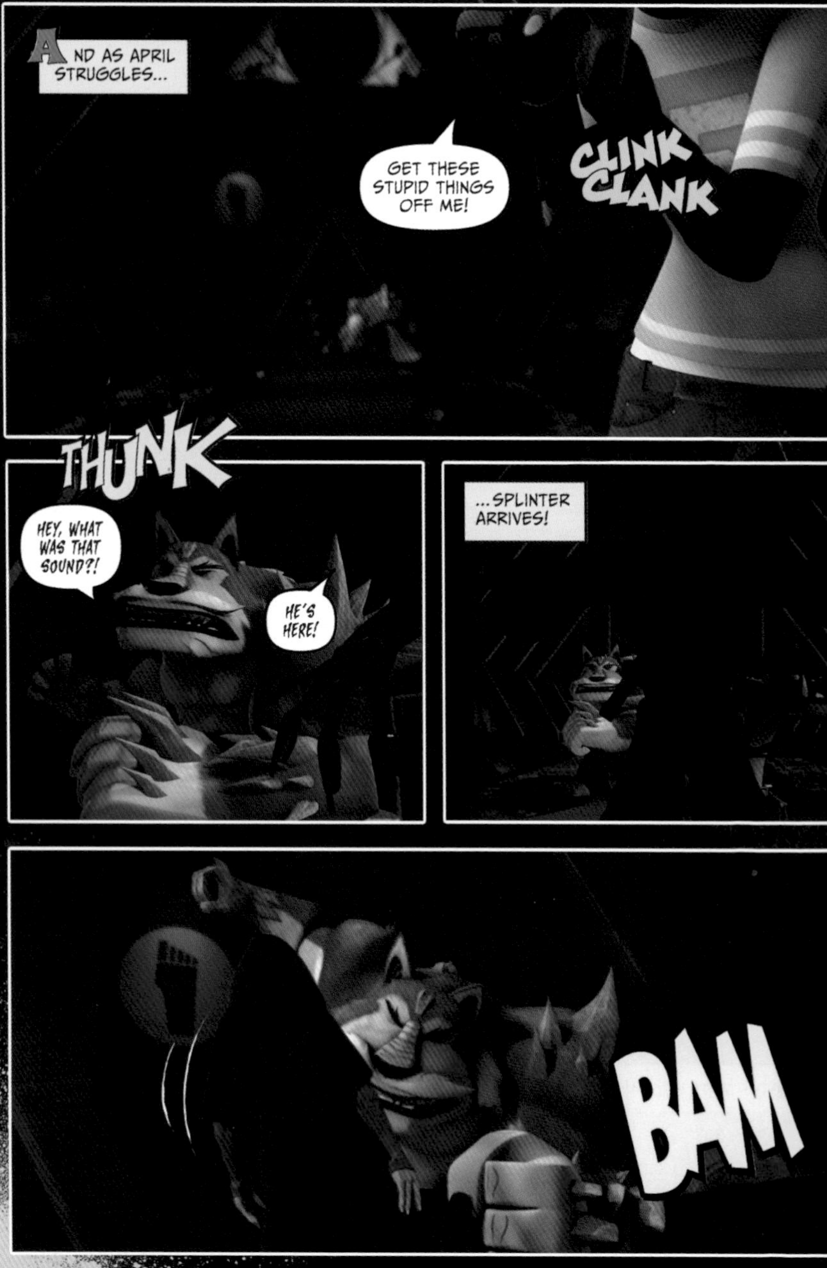
AND AS APRIL STRUGGLES...
GET THESE STUPID THINGS OFF ME!
CLINK CLANK
THUNK
HEY, WHAT WAS THAT SOUND?!
HE'S HERE!
...SPLINTER ARRIVES!
BAM

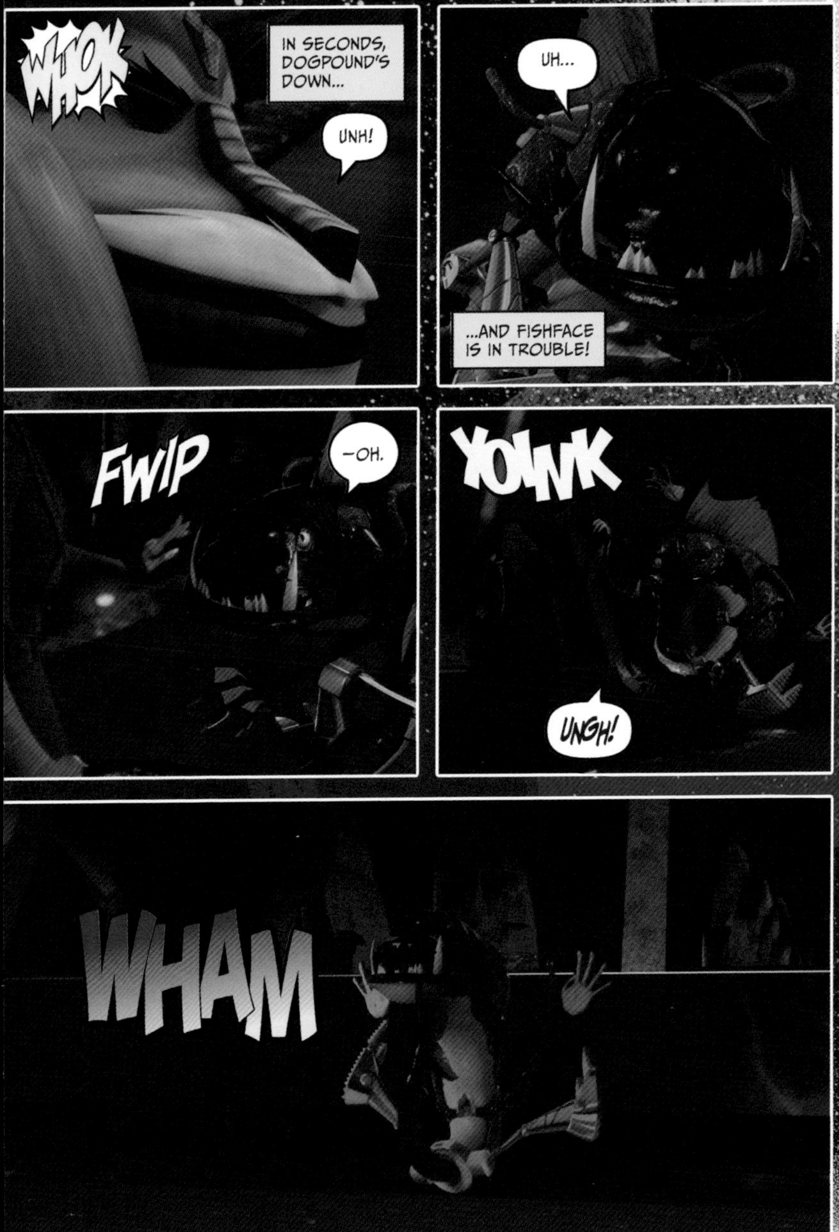
WHOK
IN SECONDS, DOGPOUND'S DOWN...
UNH!
UH...
...AND FISHFACE IS IN TROUBLE!
FWIP
-OH.
YOINK
UNGH!
WHAM

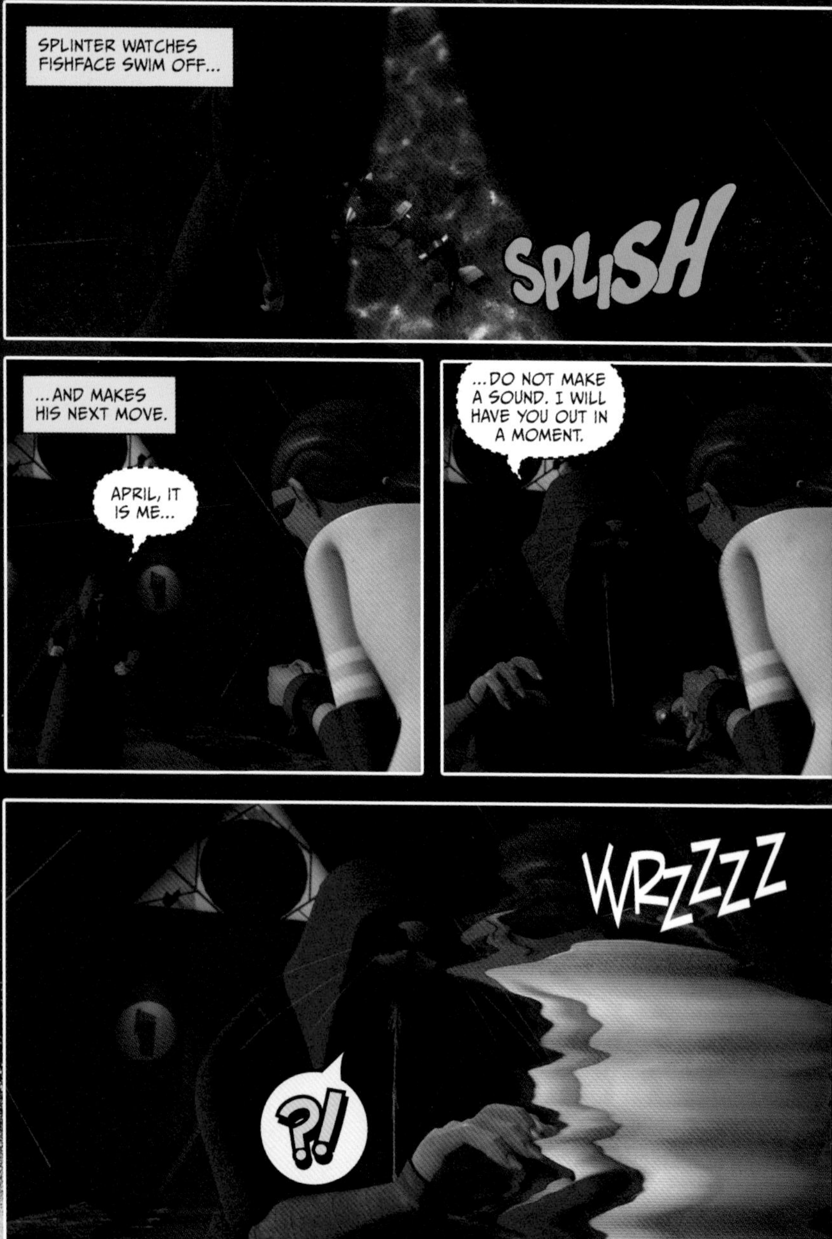
SPLINTER WATCHES FISHFACE SWIM OFF...
SPLISH
...AND MAKES HIS NEXT MOVE.
APRIL, IT IS ME...
...DO NOT MAKE A SOUND. I WILL HAVE YOU OUT IN A MOMENT.
WRZZZZ
?!

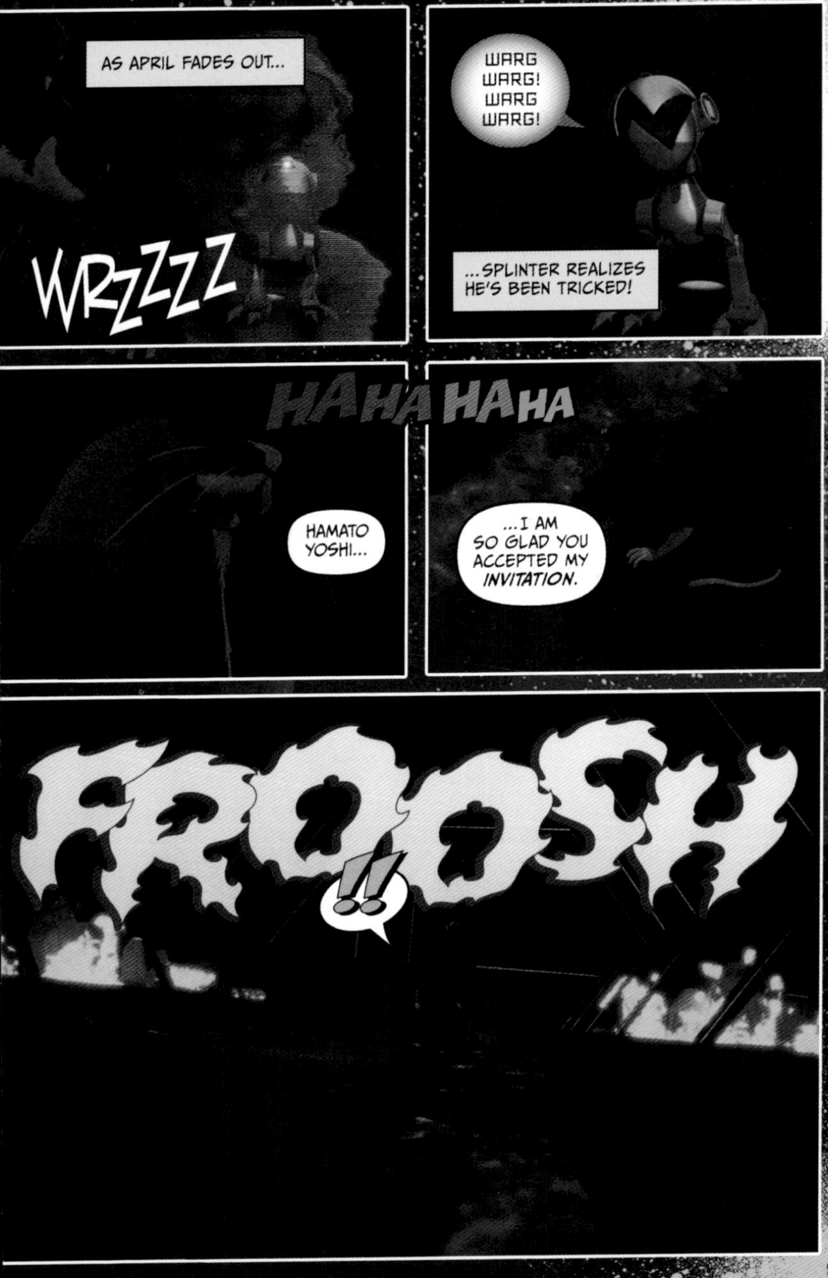
AS APRIL FADES OUT...
WRZZZZ
WARG WARG! WARG WARG!
...SPLINTER REALIZES HE'S BEEN TRICKED!
HAHAHAHAHA
HAMATO YOSHI...
...I AM SO GLAD YOU ACCEPTED MY *INVITATION*.
FROOSH
!!

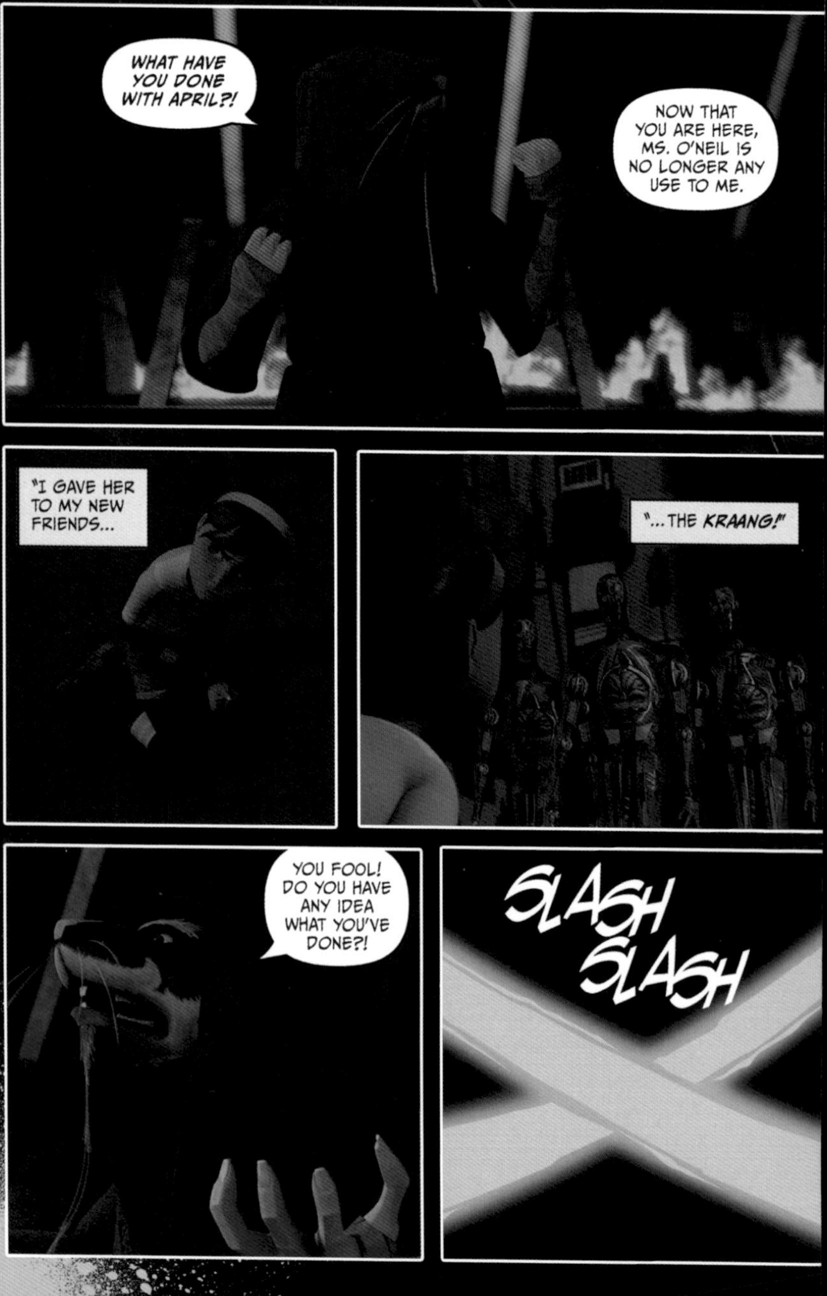
WHAT HAVE YOU DONE WITH APRIL?!
NOW THAT YOU ARE HERE, MS. O'NEIL IS NO LONGER ANY USE TO ME.
"I GAVE HER TO MY NEW FRIENDS...
"...THE KRAANG!"
YOU FOOL! DO YOU HAVE ANY IDEA WHAT YOU'VE DONE?!
SLASH
SLASH

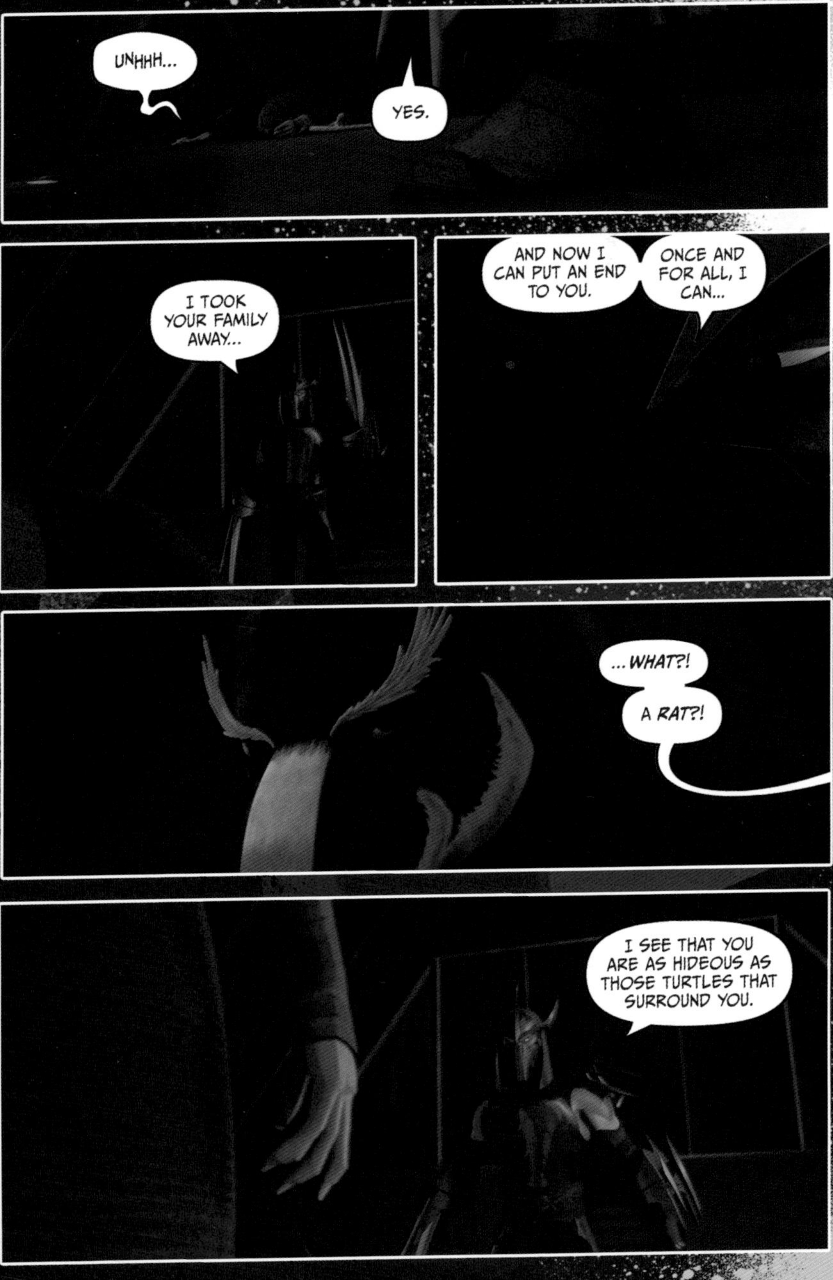
UNHHH...
YES.
I TOOK YOUR FAMILY AWAY...
AND NOW I CAN PUT AN END TO YOU.
ONCE AND FOR ALL, I CAN...
...WHAT?!
A RAT?!
I SEE THAT YOU ARE AS HIDEOUS AS THOSE TURTLES THAT SURROUND YOU.

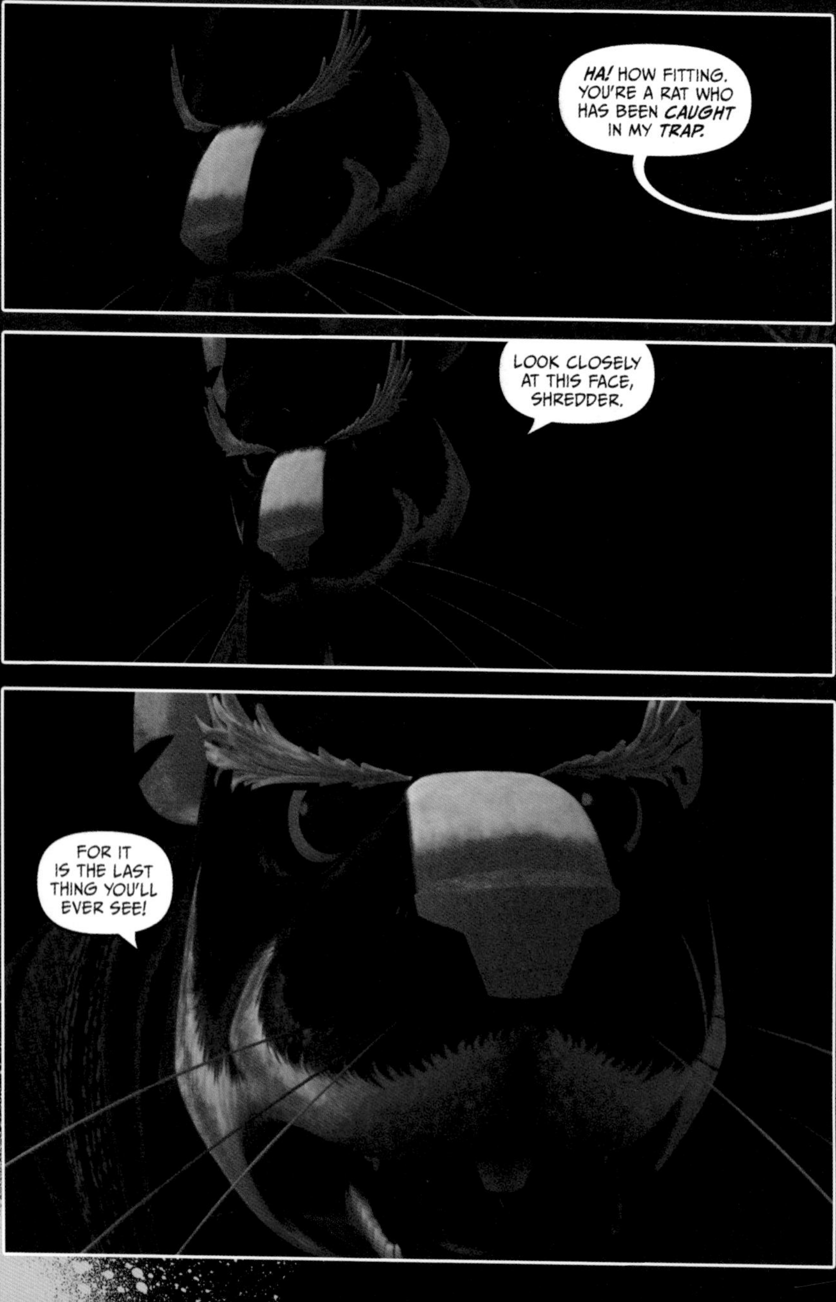
HA! HOW FITTING. YOU'RE A RAT WHO HAS BEEN CAUGHT IN MY TRAP.
LOOK CLOSELY AT THIS FACE, SHREDDER.
FOR IT IS THE LAST THING YOU'LL EVER SEE!

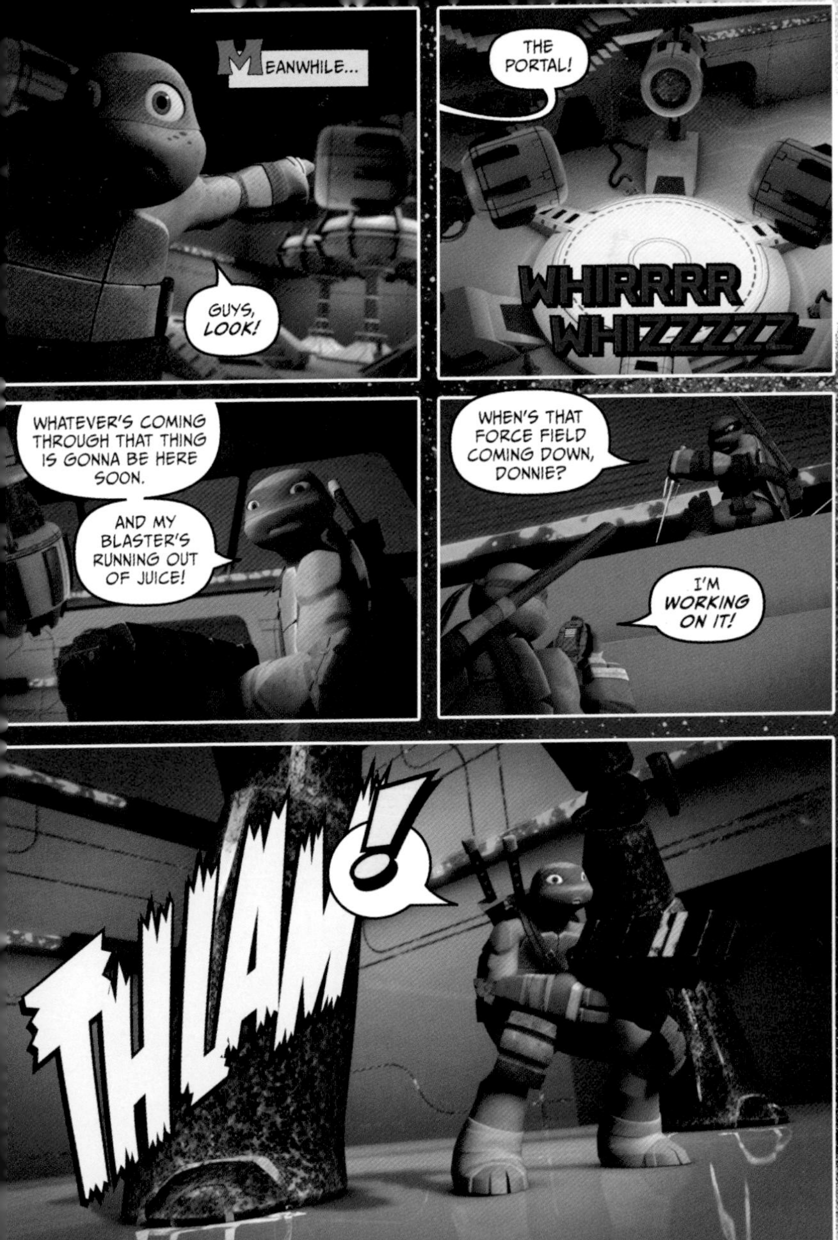
MEANWHILE...
GUYS, LOOK!
THE PORTAL!
WHIRRRR
WHIZZZZZ
WHATEVER'S COMING THROUGH THAT THING IS GONNA BE HERE SOON.
AND MY BLASTER'S RUNNING OUT OF JUICE!
WHEN'S THAT FORCE FIELD COMING DOWN, DONNIE?
I'M WORKING ON IT!
THLAM!

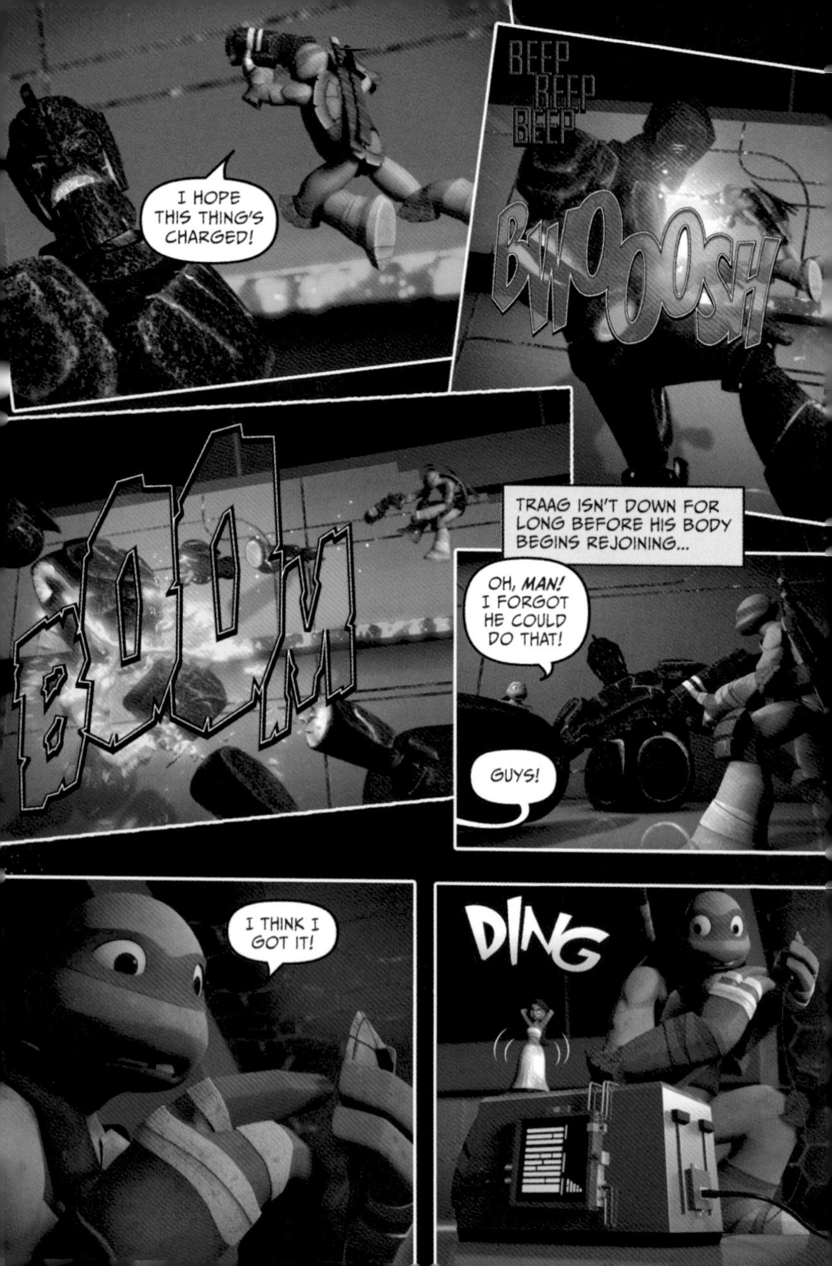
I HOPE THIS THING'S CHARGED!
BEEP BEEP BEEP
BWOOOOSH
BOOM
TRAAG ISN'T DOWN FOR LONG BEFORE HIS BODY BEGINS REJOINING...
OH, MAN! I FORGOT HE COULD DO THAT!
GUYS!
I THINK I GOT IT!
DING

WWRRRRRRRR
YES! ALL HAIL ME!
WHUMP
WHUMP
WHUMP
WHUMPWHUMP
WHUMP
...
...
...UH-OH. SORRY, GUYS.

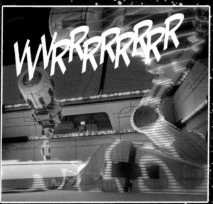

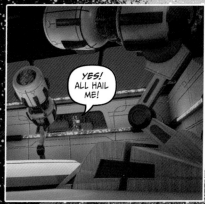

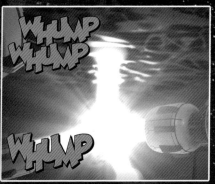

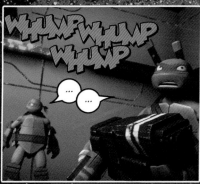

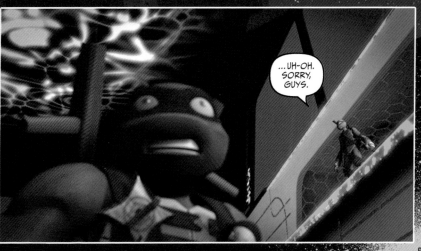

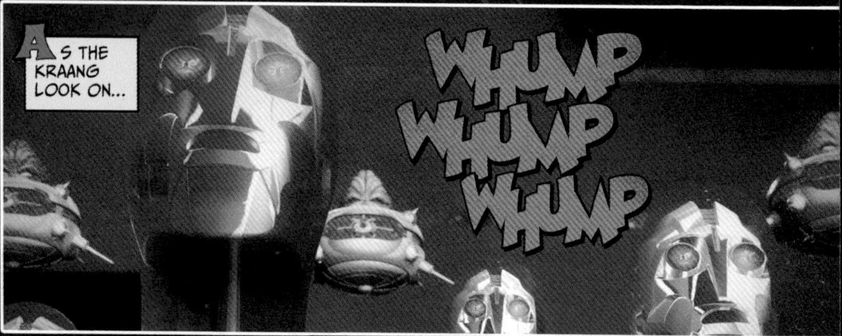
AS THE KRAANG LOOK ON...
WHUMP
WHUMP
WHUMP

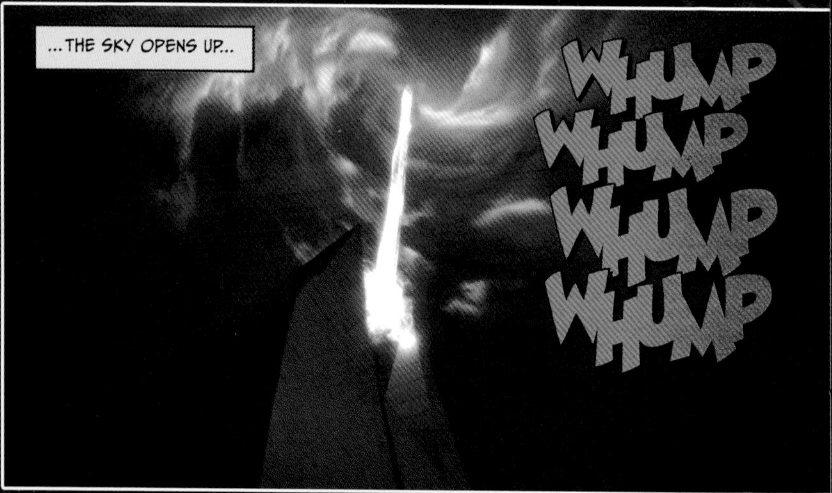
...THE SKY OPENS UP...
WHUMP
WHUMP
WHUMP
WHUMP

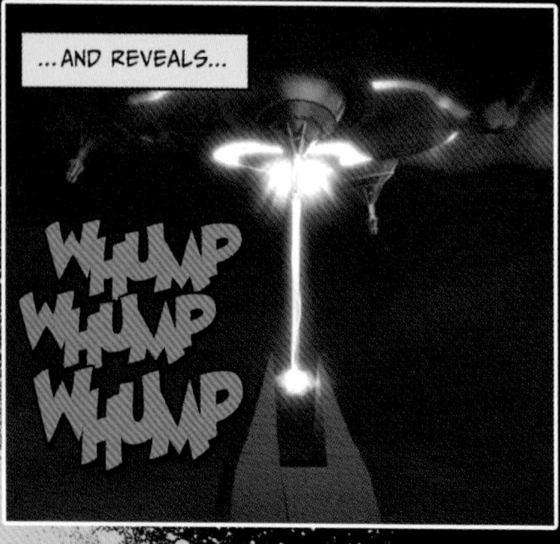
...AND REVEALS...
WHUMP
WHUMP
WHUMP

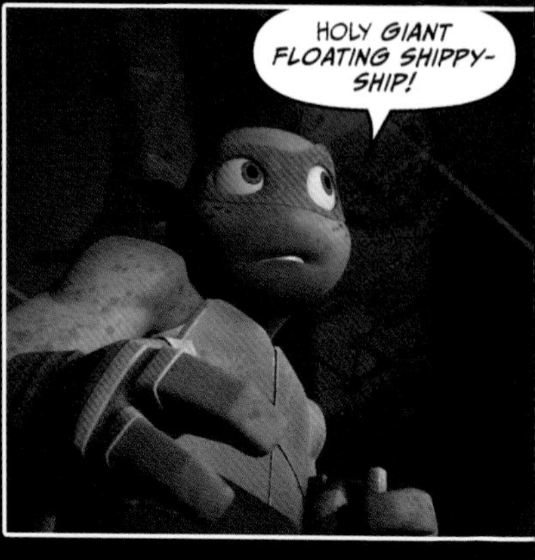
HOLY GIANT FLOATING SHIPPY-SHIP!

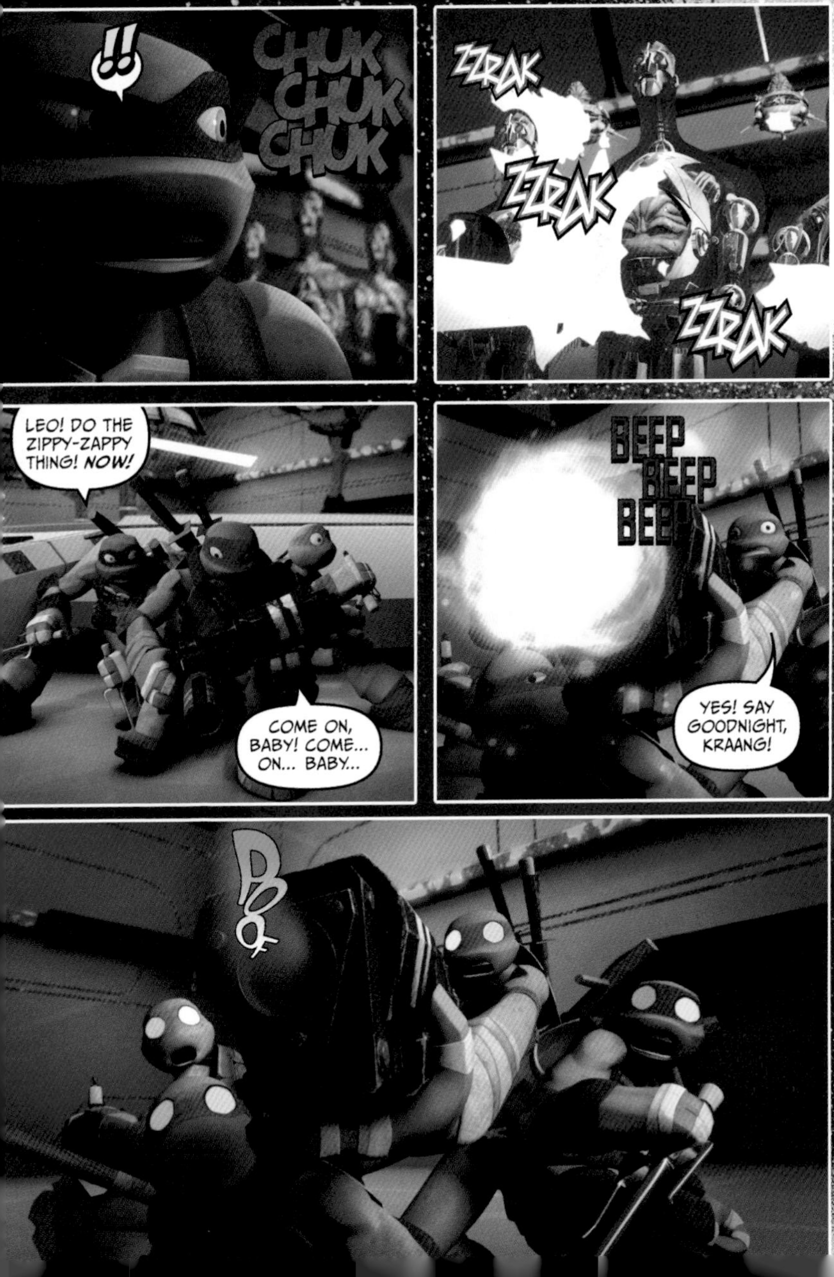
!!
CHUK CHUK CHUK
ZZRAK
Z-ZRAK
ZZRAK
LEO! DO THE ZIPPY-ZAPPY THING! NOW!
COME ON, BABY! COME... ON... BABY...
BEEP BEEP BEEP
YES! SAY GOODNIGHT, KRAANG!
BOOF

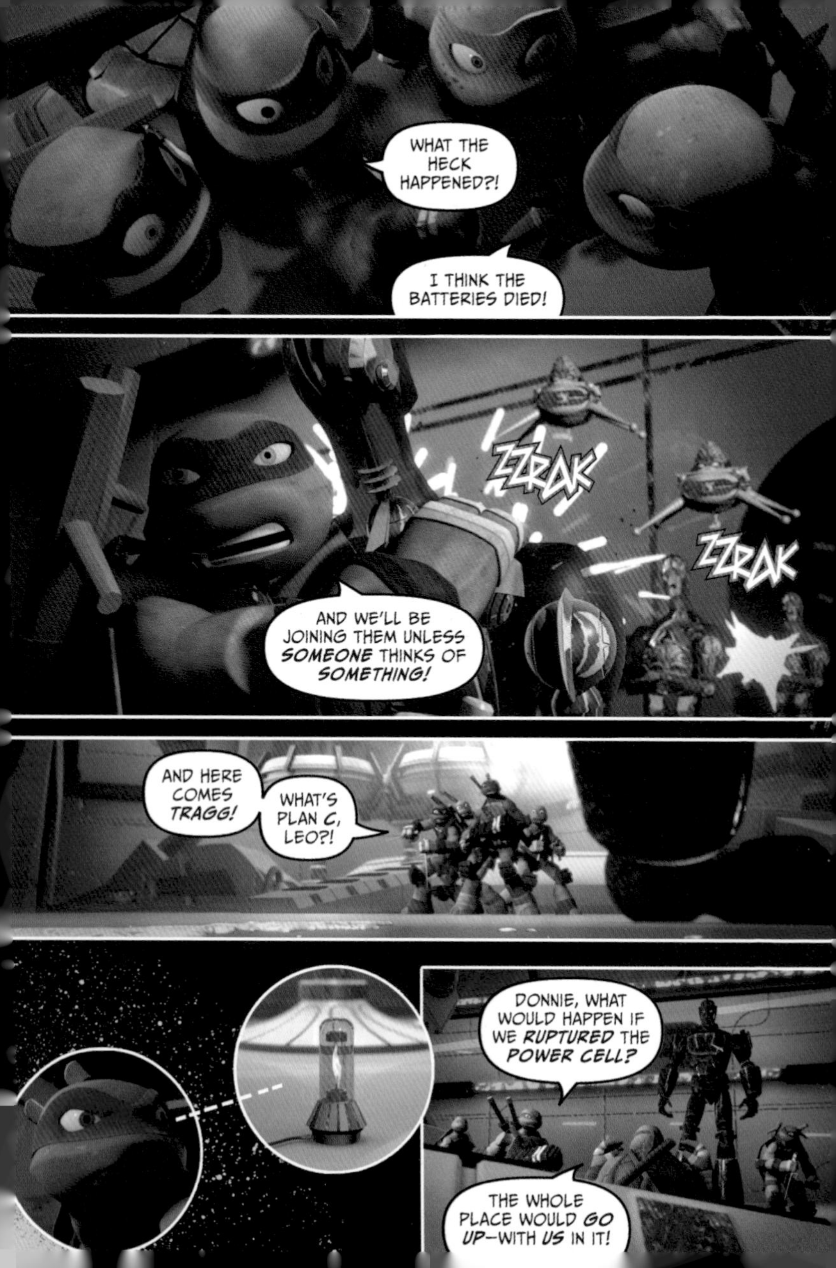
WHAT THE HECK HAPPENED?!
I THINK THE BATTERIES DIED!
ZZRAK
ZZRAK
AND WE'LL BE JOINING THEM UNLESS SOMEONE THINKS OF SOMETHING!
AND HERE COMES TRAGG!
WHAT'S PLAN C, LEO?!
DONNIE, WHAT WOULD HAPPEN IF WE RUPTURED THE POWER CELL?
THE WHOLE PLACE WOULD GO UP—WITH US IN IT!

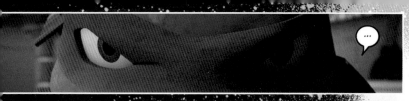

...

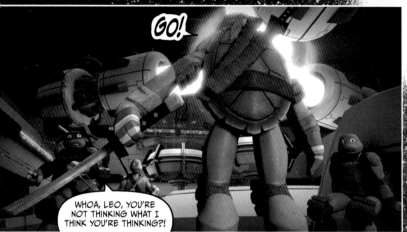

GO!

WHOA, LEO, YOU'RE NOT THINKING WHAT I THINK YOU'RE THINKING?!

HE'S THINKING IT!

LEO CUTS HIS WAY TOWARDS THE POWER CELL...

⟨HIYAAAAH!⟩

...AND STRIKES!

SHHING

BOOM

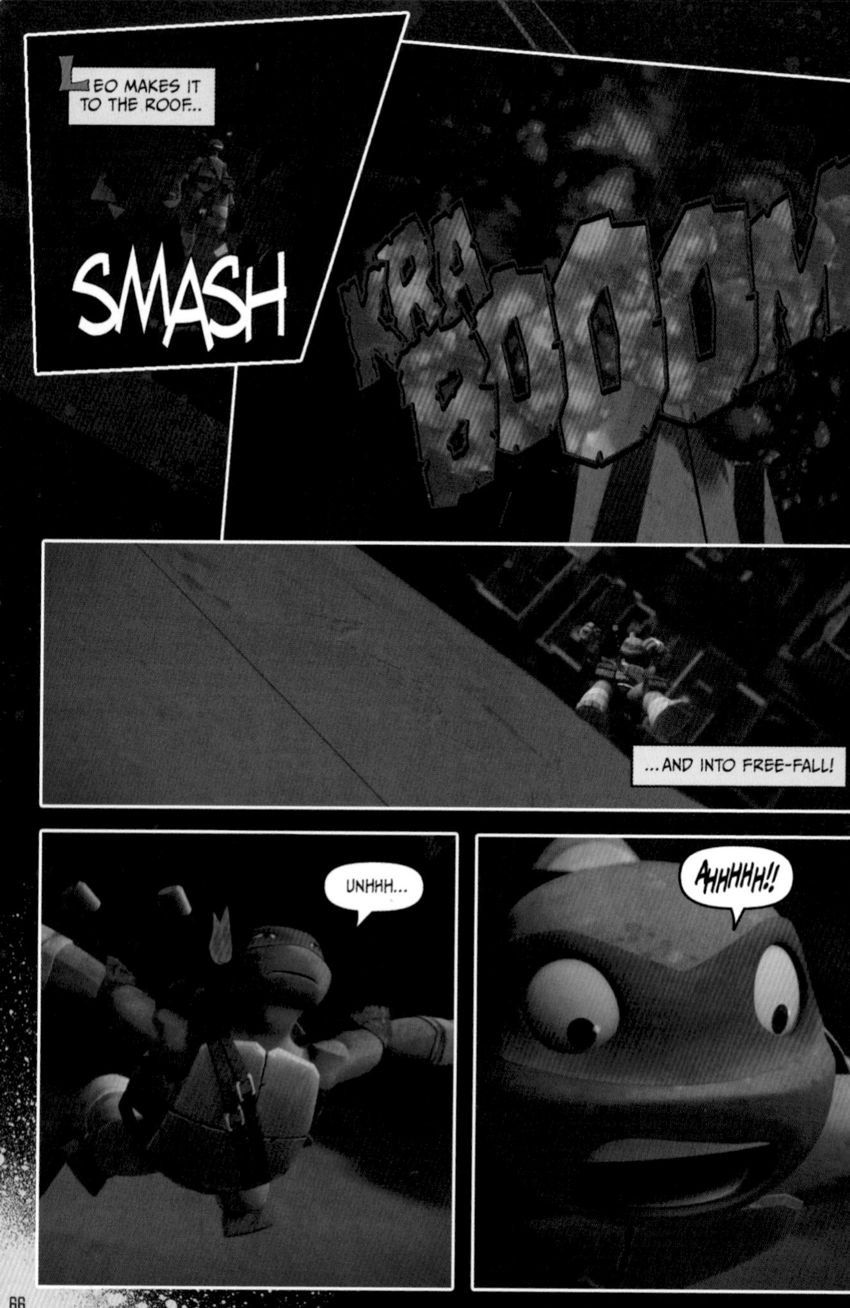
LEO MAKES IT TO THE ROOF...
SMASH
KRA-BOOOOM
...AND INTO FREE-FALL!
UNHHH...
AHHHHH!!

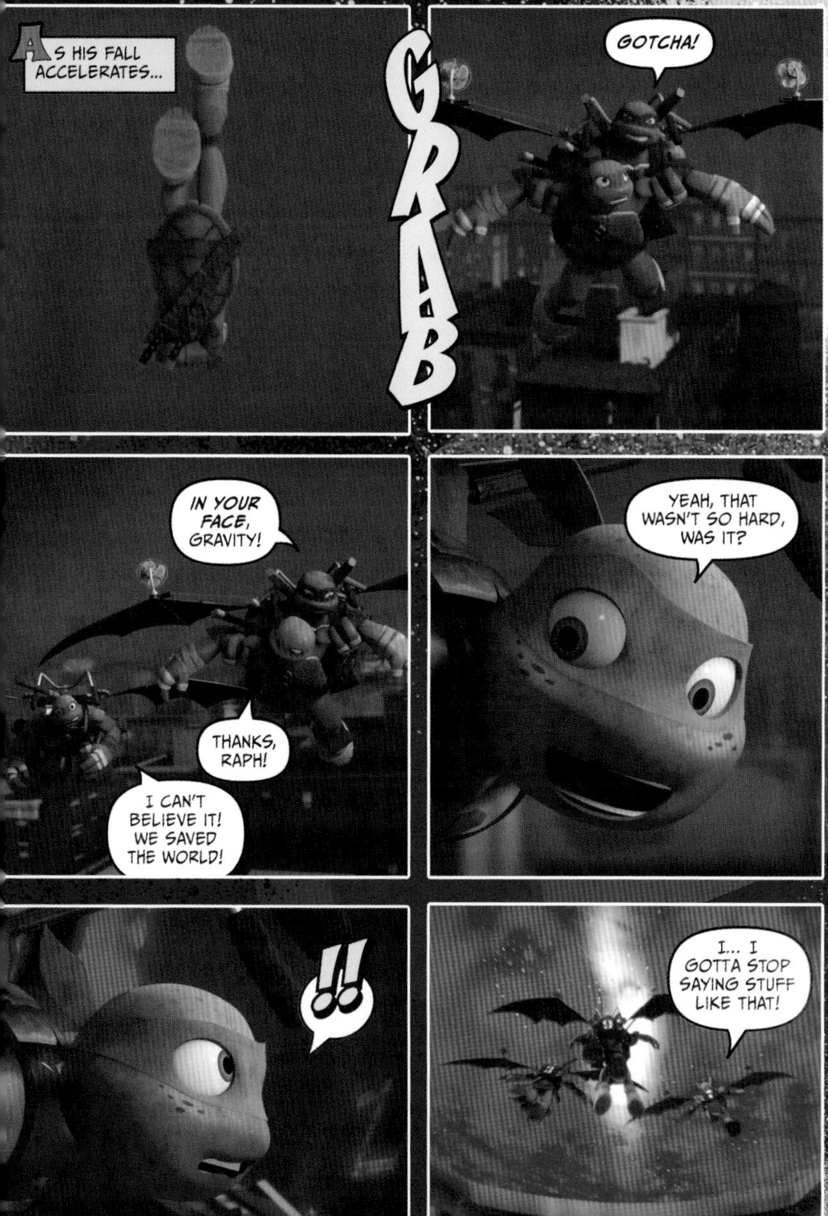

AS HIS FALL ACCELERATES...
GRAB
GOTCHA!
IN YOUR FACE, GRAVITY!
THANKS, RAPH!
I CAN'T BELIEVE IT! WE SAVED THE WORLD!
YEAH, THAT WASN'T SO HARD, WAS IT?
!!
I... I GOTTA STOP SAYING STUFF LIKE THAT!

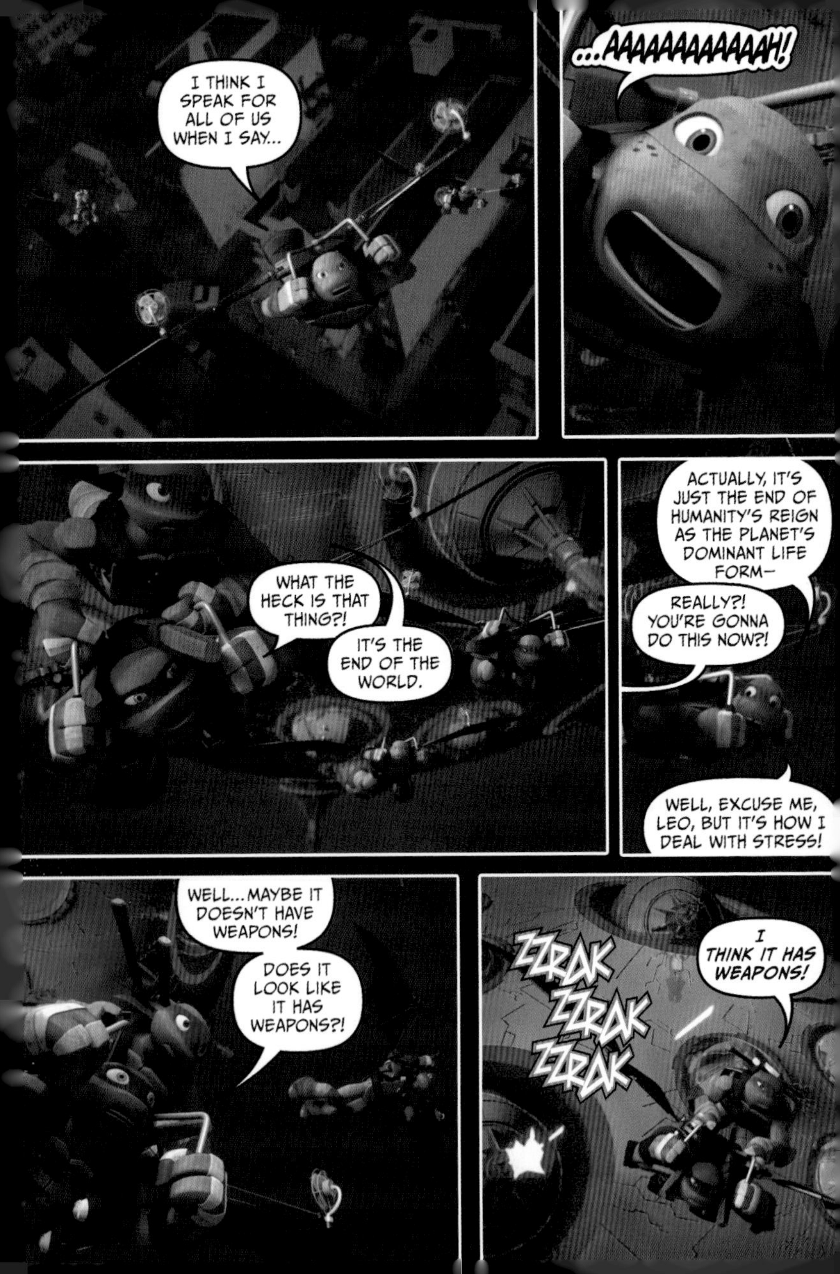
I THINK I SPEAK FOR ALL OF US WHEN I SAY...
...AAAAAAAAAAAAH!
WHAT THE HECK IS THAT THING?!
IT'S THE END OF THE WORLD.
ACTUALLY, IT'S JUST THE END OF HUMANITY'S REIGN AS THE PLANET'S DOMINANT LIFE FORM—
REALLY?! YOU'RE GONNA DO THIS NOW?!
WELL, EXCUSE ME, LEO, BUT IT'S HOW I DEAL WITH STRESS!
WELL...MAYBE IT DOESN'T HAVE WEAPONS!
DOES IT LOOK LIKE IT HAS WEAPONS?!
ZZRAK
ZZRAK
ZZRAK
I THINK IT HAS WEAPONS!

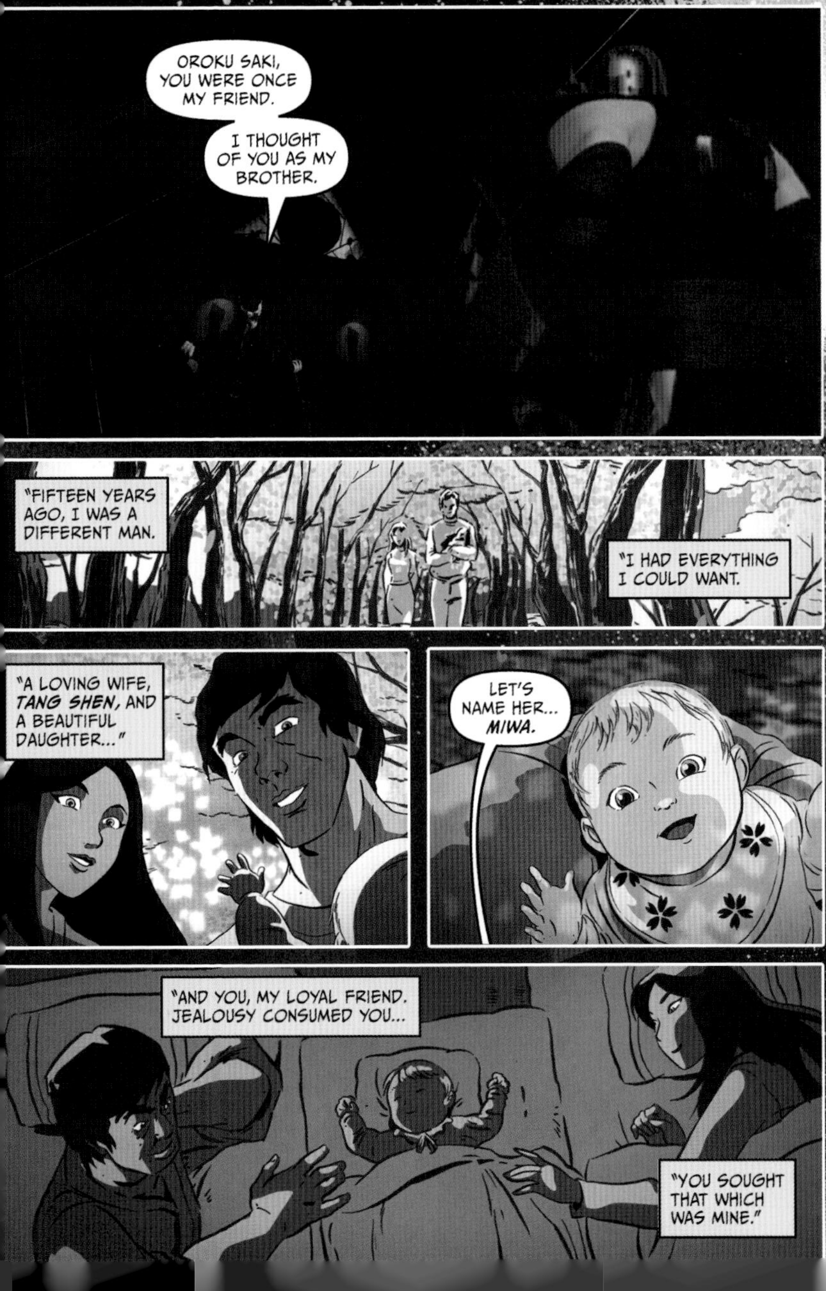

OROKU SAKI, YOU WERE ONCE MY FRIEND.
I THOUGHT OF YOU AS MY BROTHER.
"FIFTEEN YEARS AGO, I WAS A DIFFERENT MAN.
"I HAD EVERYTHING I COULD WANT.
"A LOVING WIFE, ***TANG SHEN,*** AND A BEAUTIFUL DAUGHTER..."
LET'S NAME HER... ***MIWA.***
"AND YOU, MY LOYAL FRIEND. JEALOUSY CONSUMED YOU...
"YOU SOUGHT THAT WHICH WAS MINE."

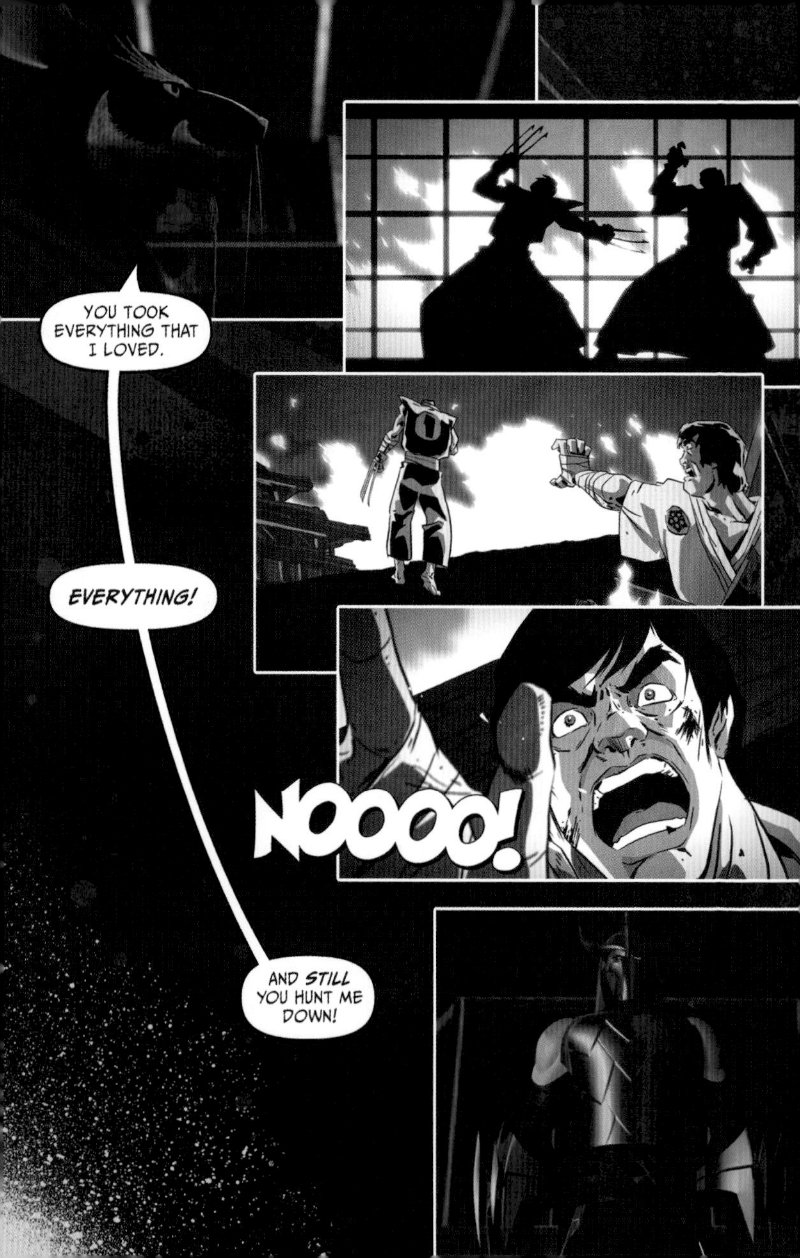
YOU TOOK EVERYTHING THAT I LOVED.
EVERYTHING!
NOOOO!
AND STILL YOU HUNT ME DOWN!

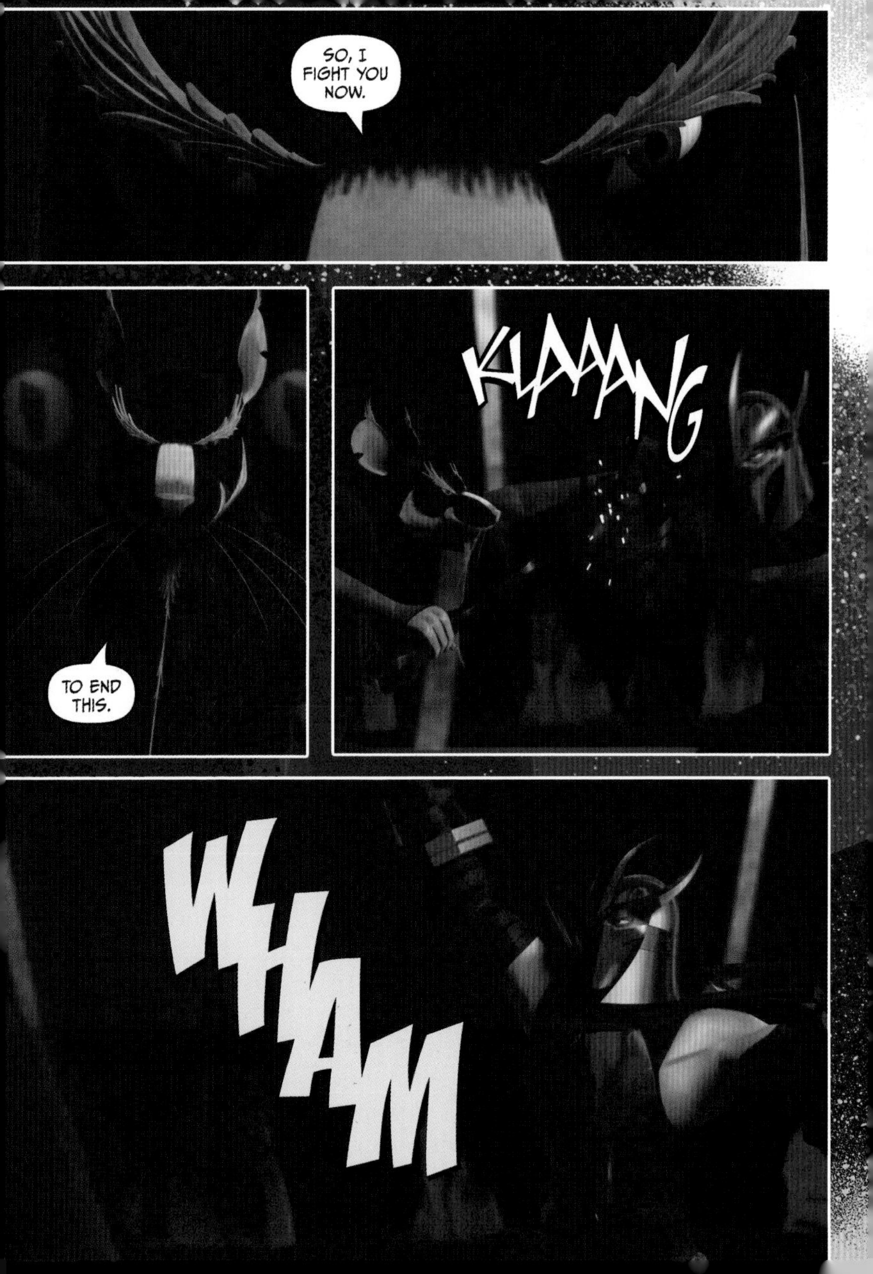
SO, I FIGHT YOU NOW.
TO END THIS.
KLAAANG
WHAM

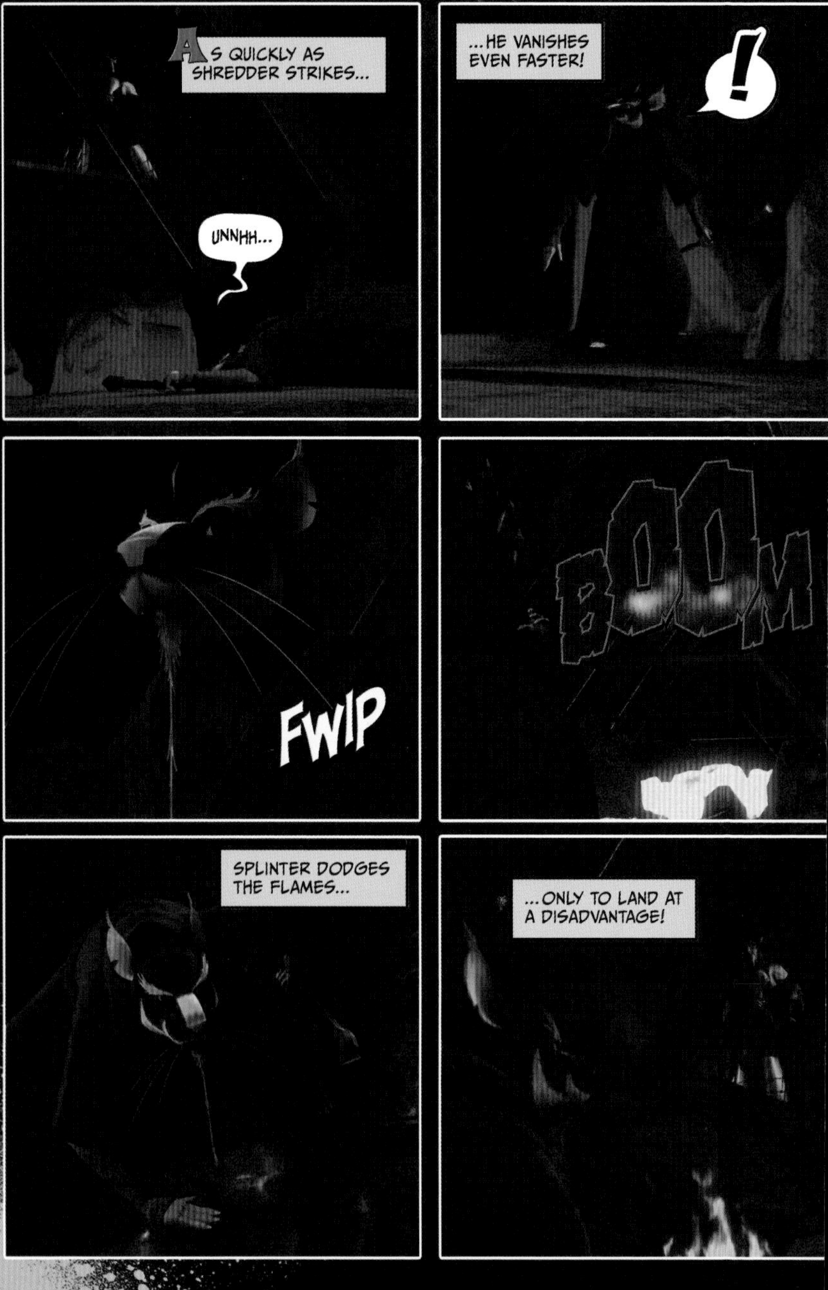
AS QUICKLY AS SHREDDER STRIKES...
UNNHH...
...HE VANISHES EVEN FASTER!
!
FWIP
BOOM
SPLINTER DODGES THE FLAMES...
...ONLY TO LAND AT A DISADVANTAGE!

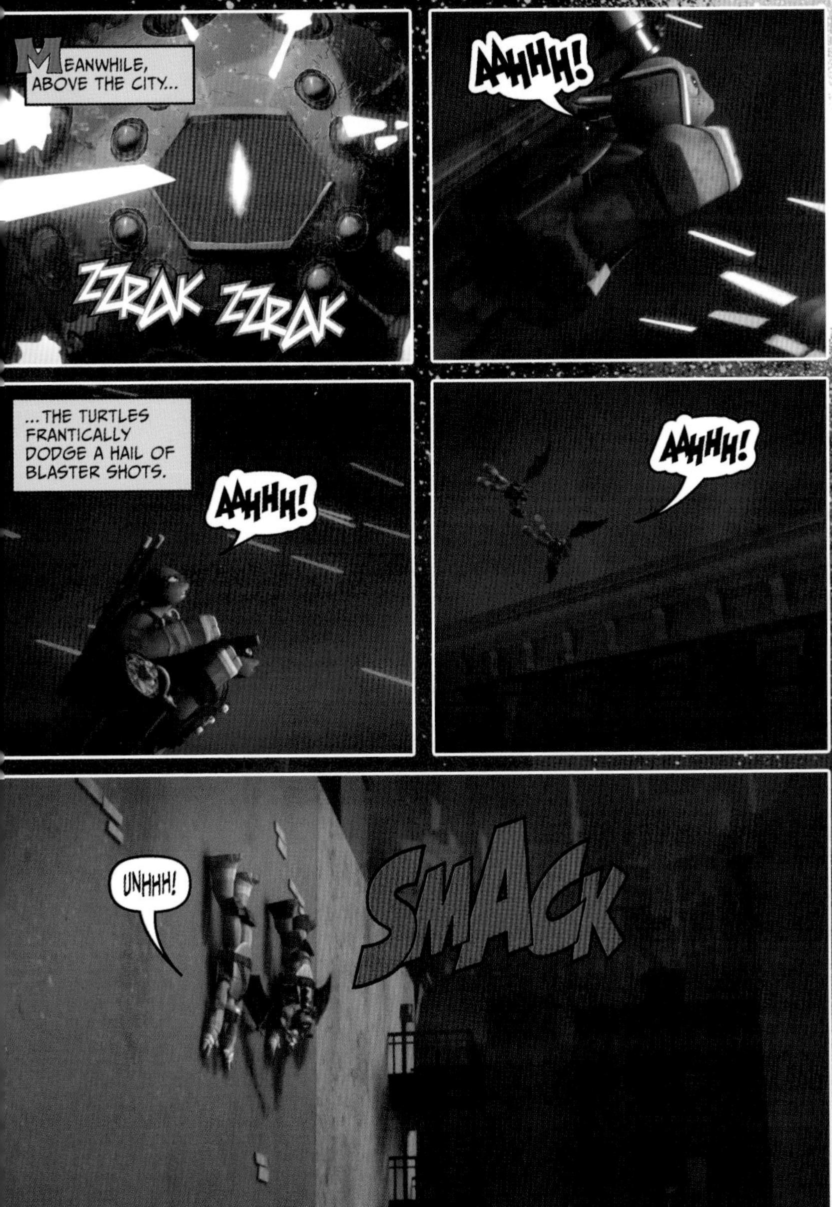
MEANWHILE, ABOVE THE CITY...
ZZRAK ZZRAK
AAHHH!
...THE TURTLES FRANTICALLY DODGE A HAIL OF BLASTER SHOTS.
AAHHH!
AAHHH!
UNHHH!
SMACK

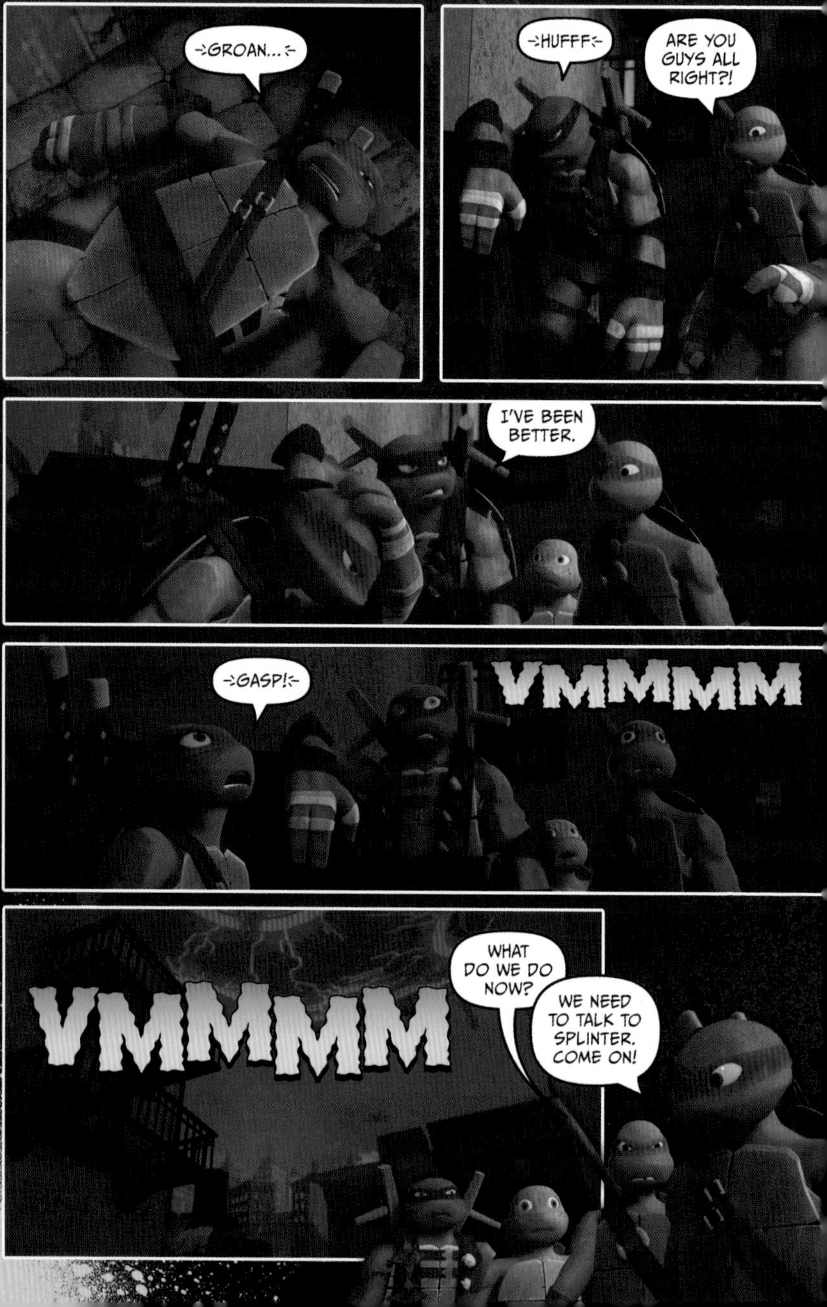

-GROAN...-
-HUFFF-
ARE YOU GUYS ALL RIGHT?!
I'VE BEEN BETTER.
-GASP!-
VMMMMM
VMMMM
WHAT DO WE DO NOW?
WE NEED TO TALK TO SPLINTER. COME ON!

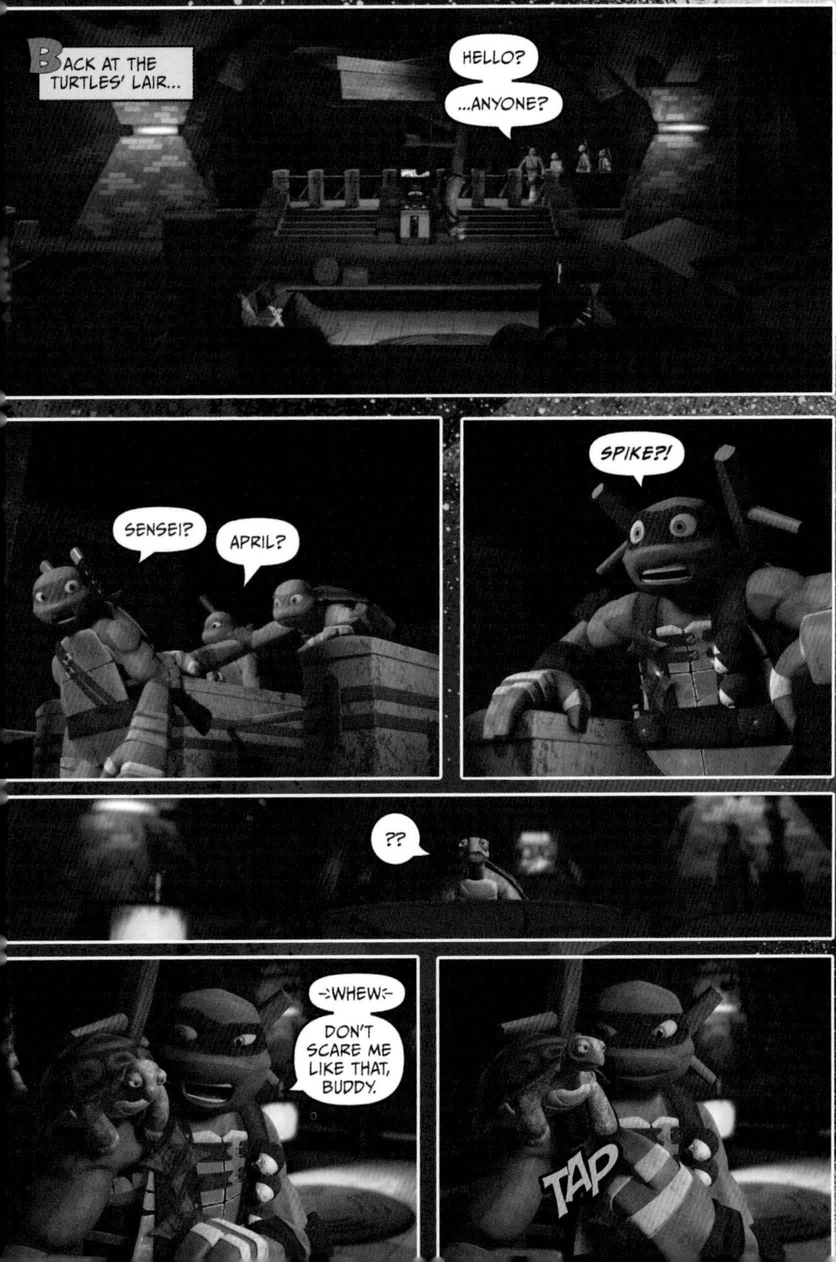
BACK AT THE TURTLES' LAIR...
HELLO?
...ANYONE?
SENSEI?
APRIL?
SPIKE?!
??
WHEW
DON'T SCARE ME LIKE THAT, BUDDY.
TAP

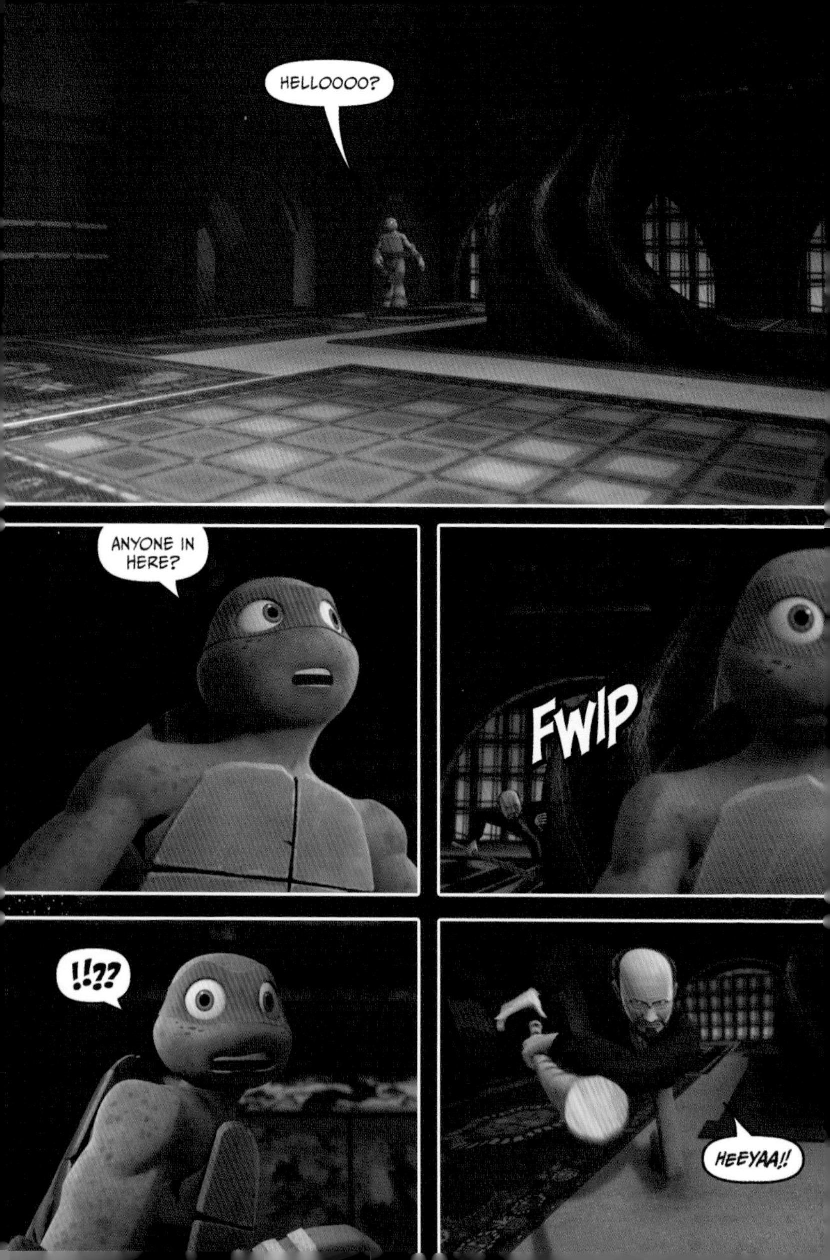
HELLOOOO?
ANYONE IN HERE?
FWIP
!!??
HEEYAA!!

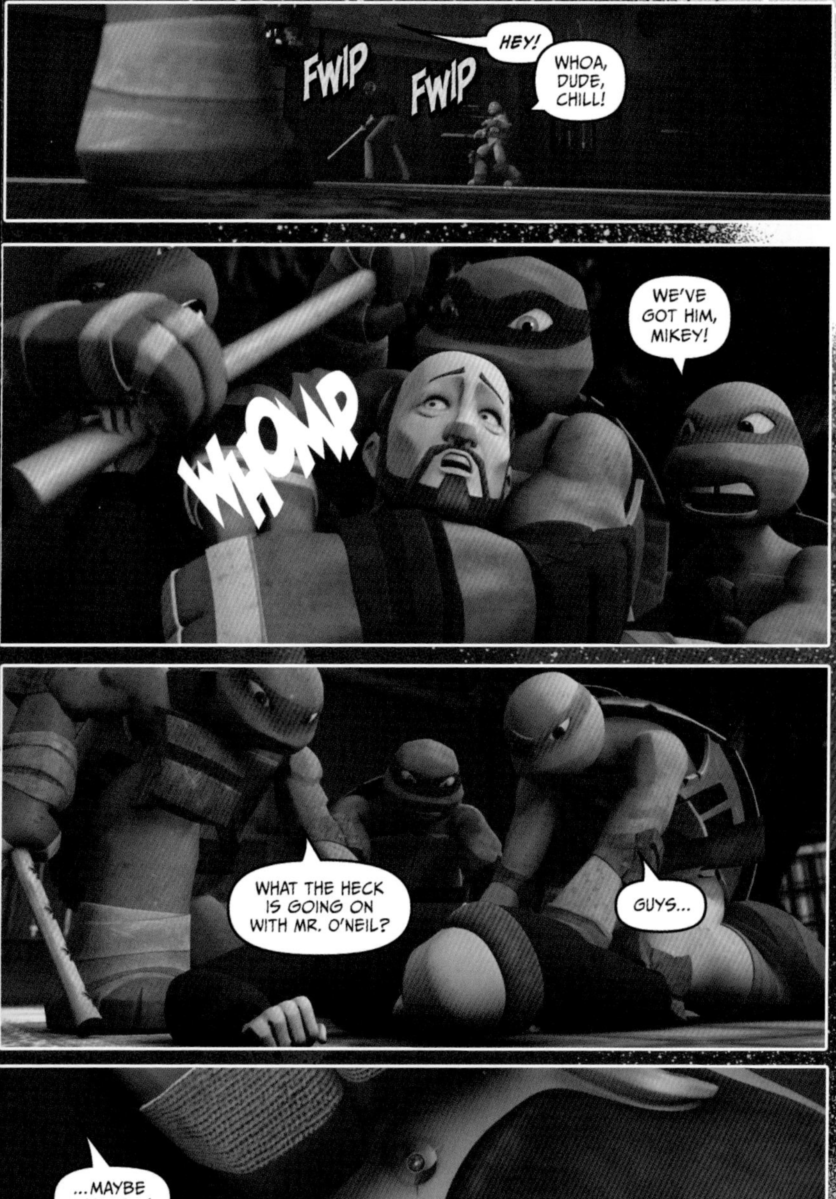
FWIP
FWIP
HEY!
WHOA, DUDE, CHILL!
WE'VE GOT HIM, MIKEY!
WHOMP
WHAT THE HECK IS GOING ON WITH MR. O'NEIL?
GUYS...
...MAYBE IT'S *THIS!*

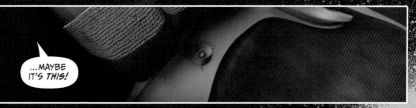

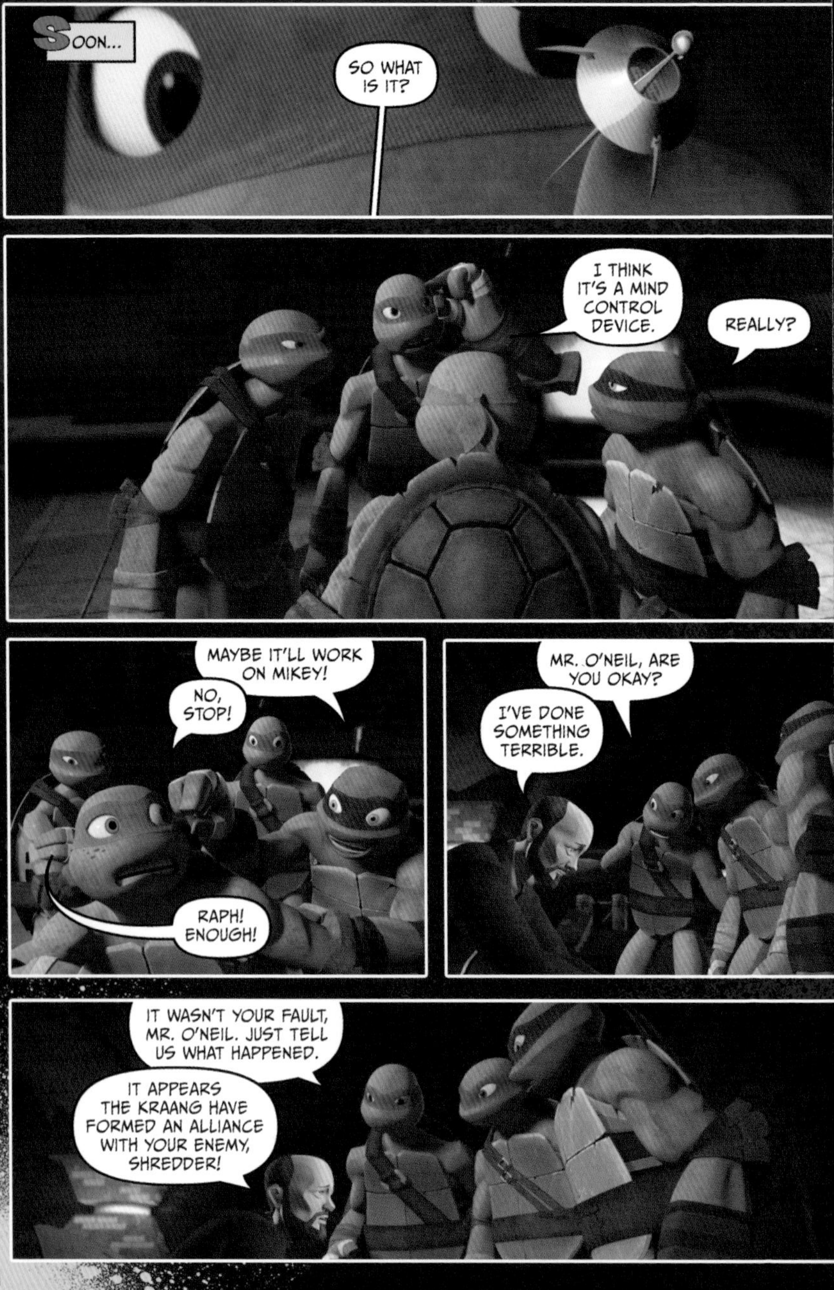
SOON...
SO WHAT IS IT?
I THINK IT'S A MIND CONTROL DEVICE.
REALLY?
MAYBE IT'LL WORK ON MIKEY!
NO, STOP!
RAPH! ENOUGH!
MR. O'NEIL, ARE YOU OKAY?
I'VE DONE SOMETHING TERRIBLE.
IT WASN'T YOUR FAULT, MR. O'NEIL. JUST TELL US WHAT HAPPENED.
IT APPEARS THE KRAANG HAVE FORMED AN ALLIANCE WITH YOUR ENEMY, SHREDDER!

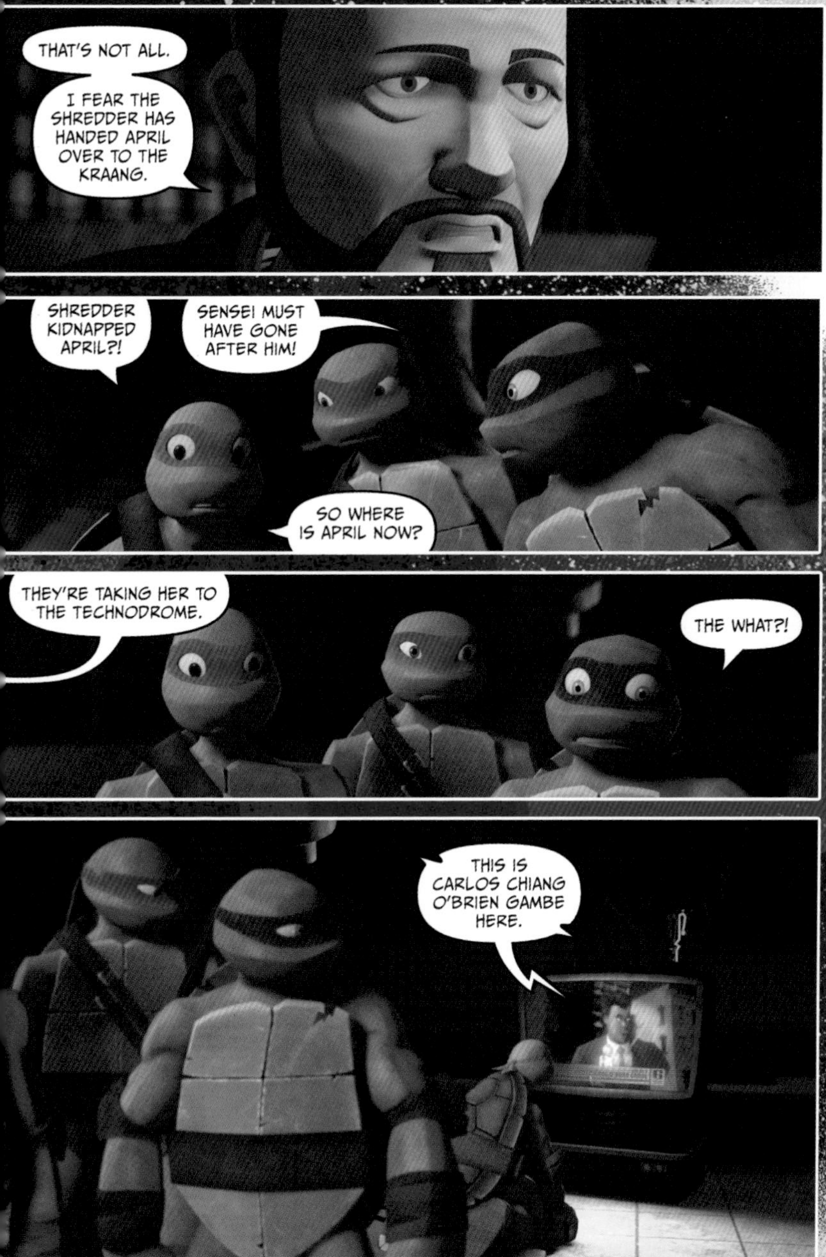
THAT'S NOT ALL.
I FEAR THE SHREDDER HAS HANDED APRIL OVER TO THE KRAANG.
SHREDDER KIDNAPPED APRIL?!
SENSEI MUST HAVE GONE AFTER HIM!
SO WHERE IS APRIL NOW?
THEY'RE TAKING HER TO THE TECHNODROME.
THE WHAT?!
THIS IS CARLOS CHIANG O'BRIEN GAMBE HERE.

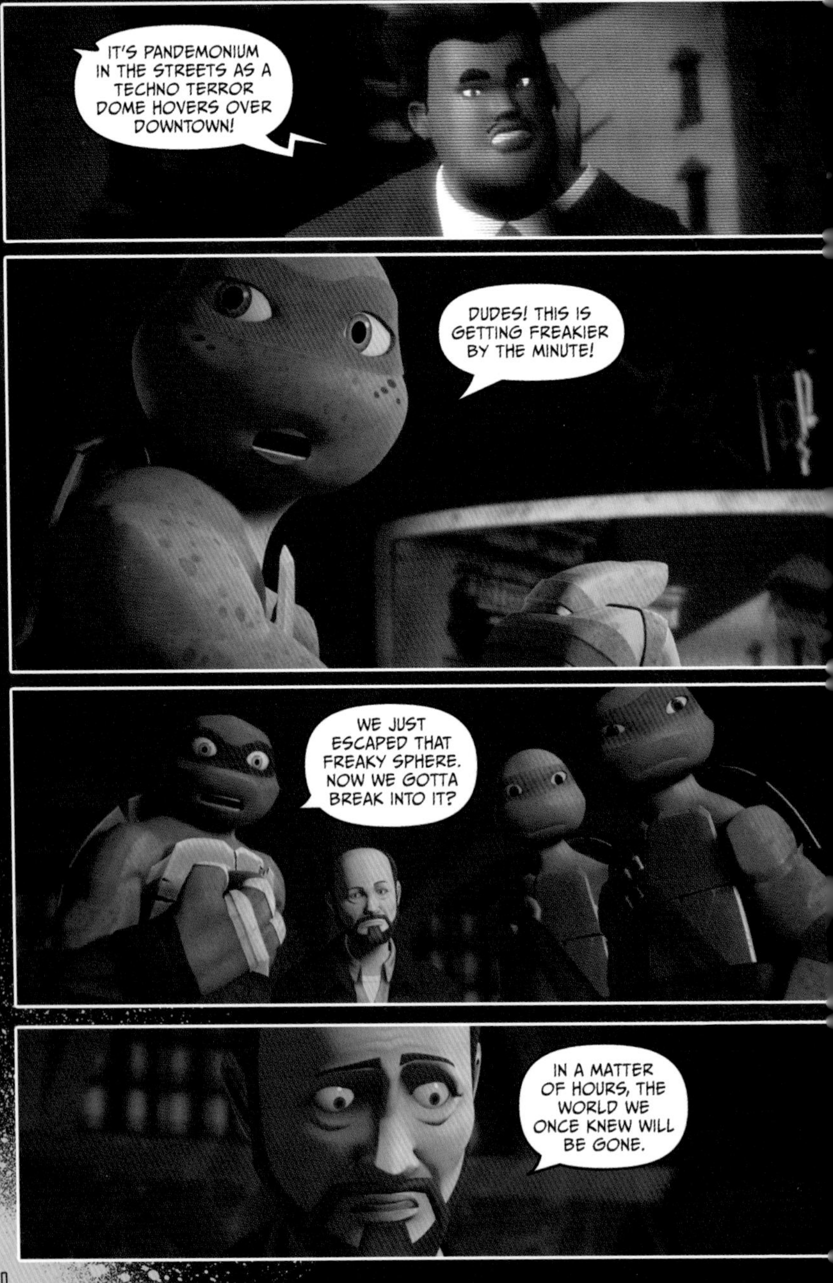
IT'S PANDEMONIUM IN THE STREETS AS A TECHNO TERROR DOME HOVERS OVER DOWNTOWN!
DUDES! THIS IS GETTING FREAKIER BY THE MINUTE!
WE JUST ESCAPED THAT FREAKY SPHERE. NOW WE GOTTA BREAK INTO IT?
IN A MATTER OF HOURS, THE WORLD WE ONCE KNEW WILL BE GONE.

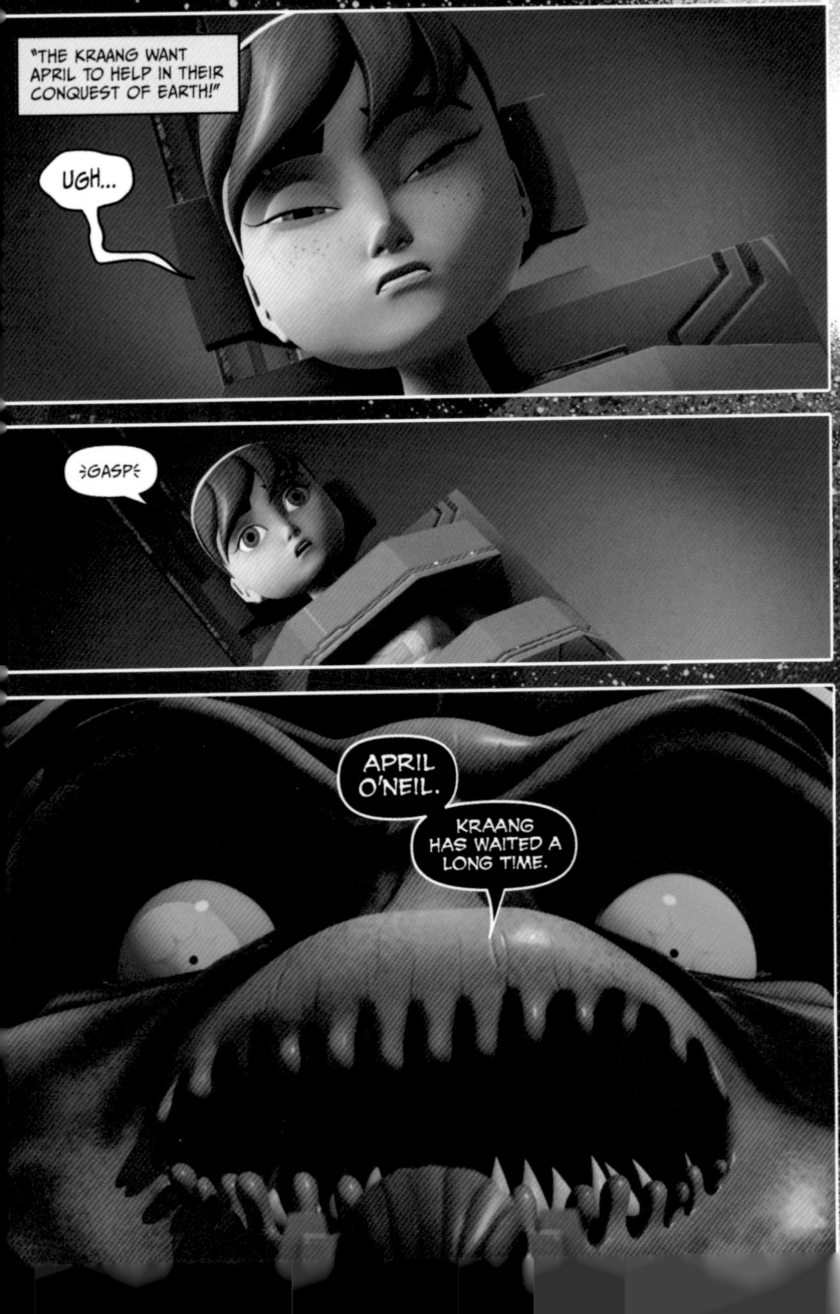
"THE KRAANG WANT APRIL TO HELP IN THEIR CONQUEST OF EARTH!"
UGH...
GASP
APRIL O'NEIL.
KRAANG HAS WAITED A LONG TIME.

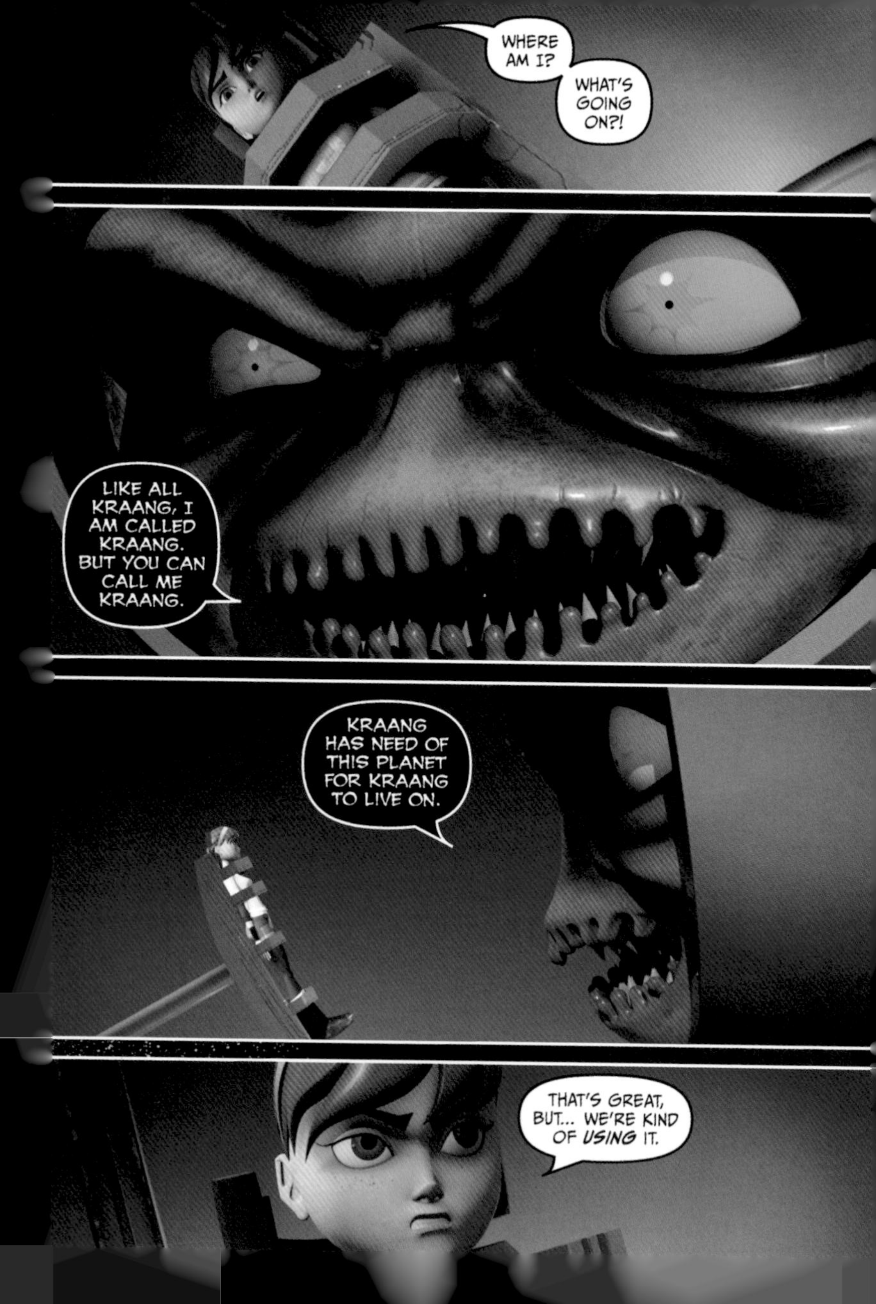
WHERE AM I?
WHAT'S GOING ON?!
LIKE ALL KRAANG, I AM CALLED KRAANG. BUT YOU CAN CALL ME KRAANG.
KRAANG HAS NEED OF THIS PLANET FOR KRAANG TO LIVE ON.
THAT'S GREAT, BUT... WE'RE KIND OF *USING* IT.

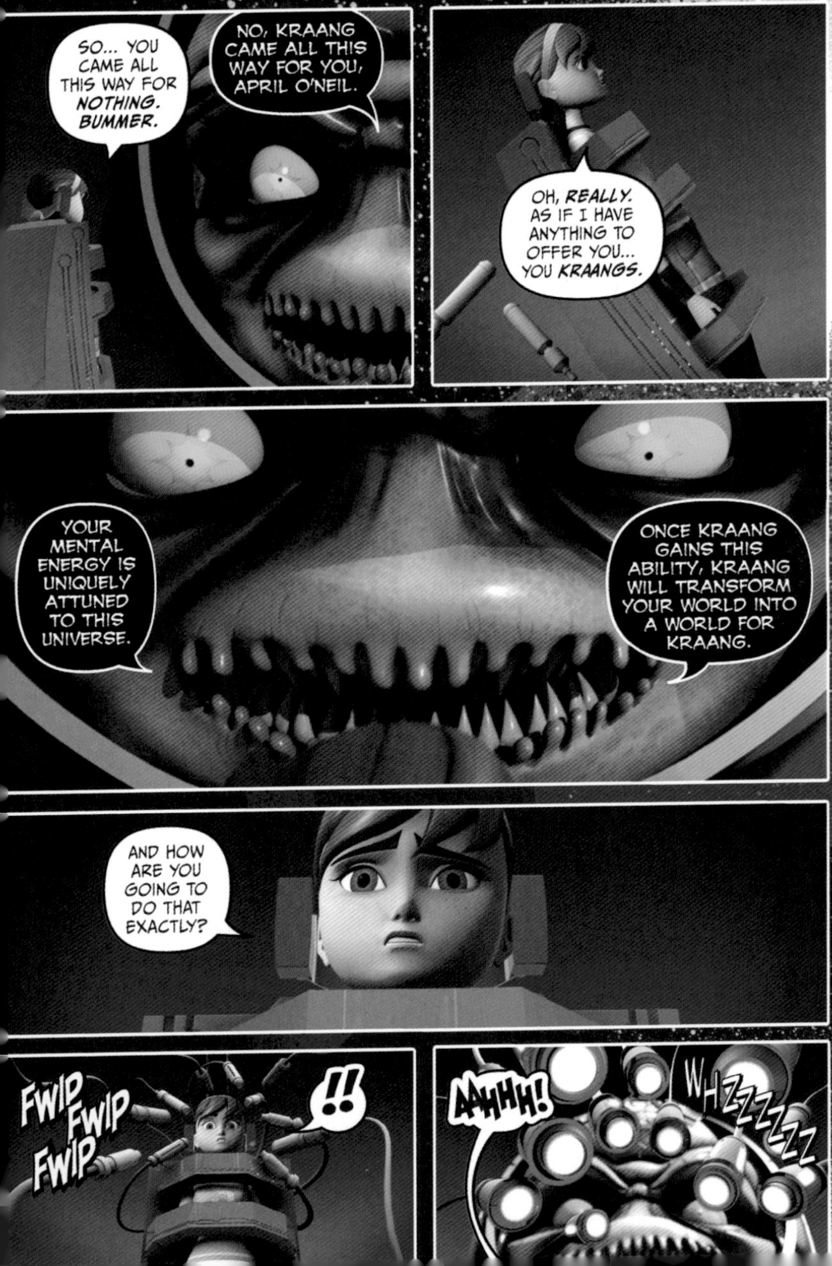

SO... YOU CAME ALL THIS WAY FOR NOTHING. BUMMER.
NO, KRAANG CAME ALL THIS WAY FOR YOU, APRIL O'NEIL.
OH, REALLY. AS IF I HAVE ANYTHING TO OFFER YOU... YOU KRAANGS.
YOUR MENTAL ENERGY IS UNIQUELY ATTUNED TO THIS UNIVERSE.
ONCE KRAANG GAINS THIS ABILITY, KRAANG WILL TRANSFORM YOUR WORLD INTO A WORLD FOR KRAANG.
AND HOW ARE YOU GOING TO DO THAT EXACTLY?
FWIP FWIP FWIP
!!
AAHHH!
WHZZZZZZZ

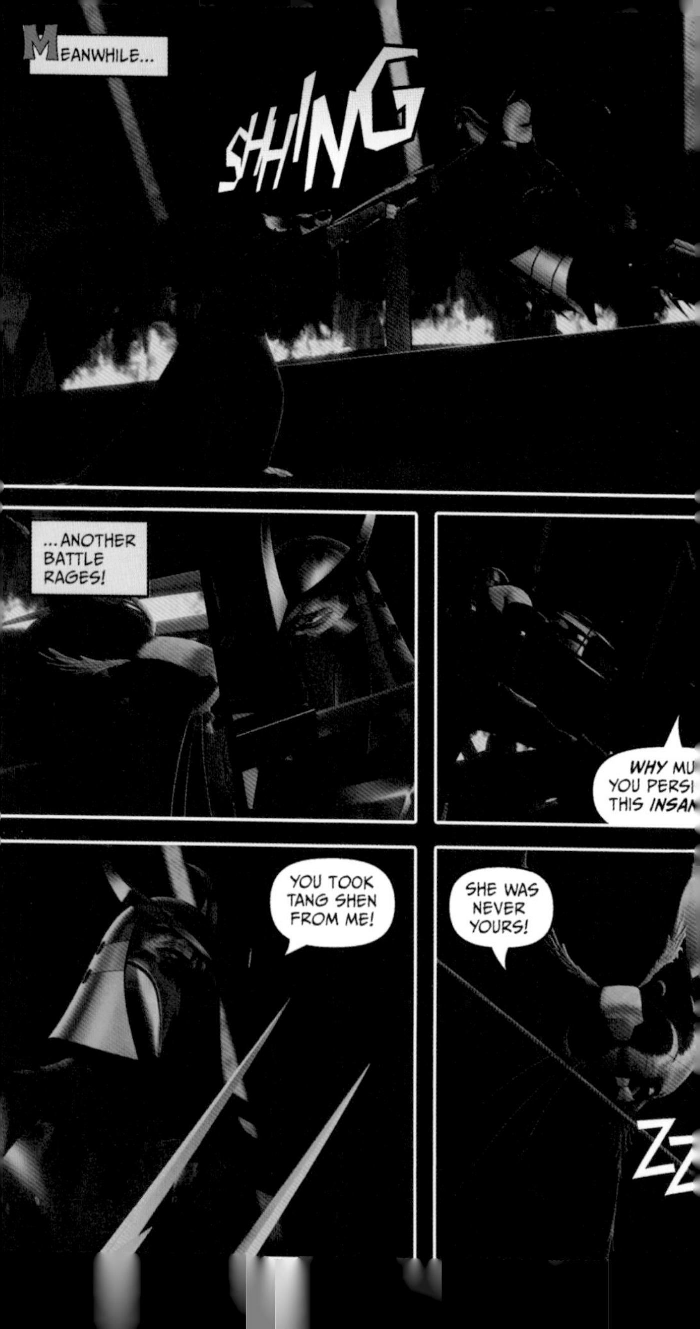
MEANWHILE...
SHHING
...ANOTHER BATTLE RAGES!
WHY MU
YOU PERSI
THIS INSAN
YOU TOOK TANG SHEN FROM ME!
SHE WAS NEVER YOURS!
ZZ

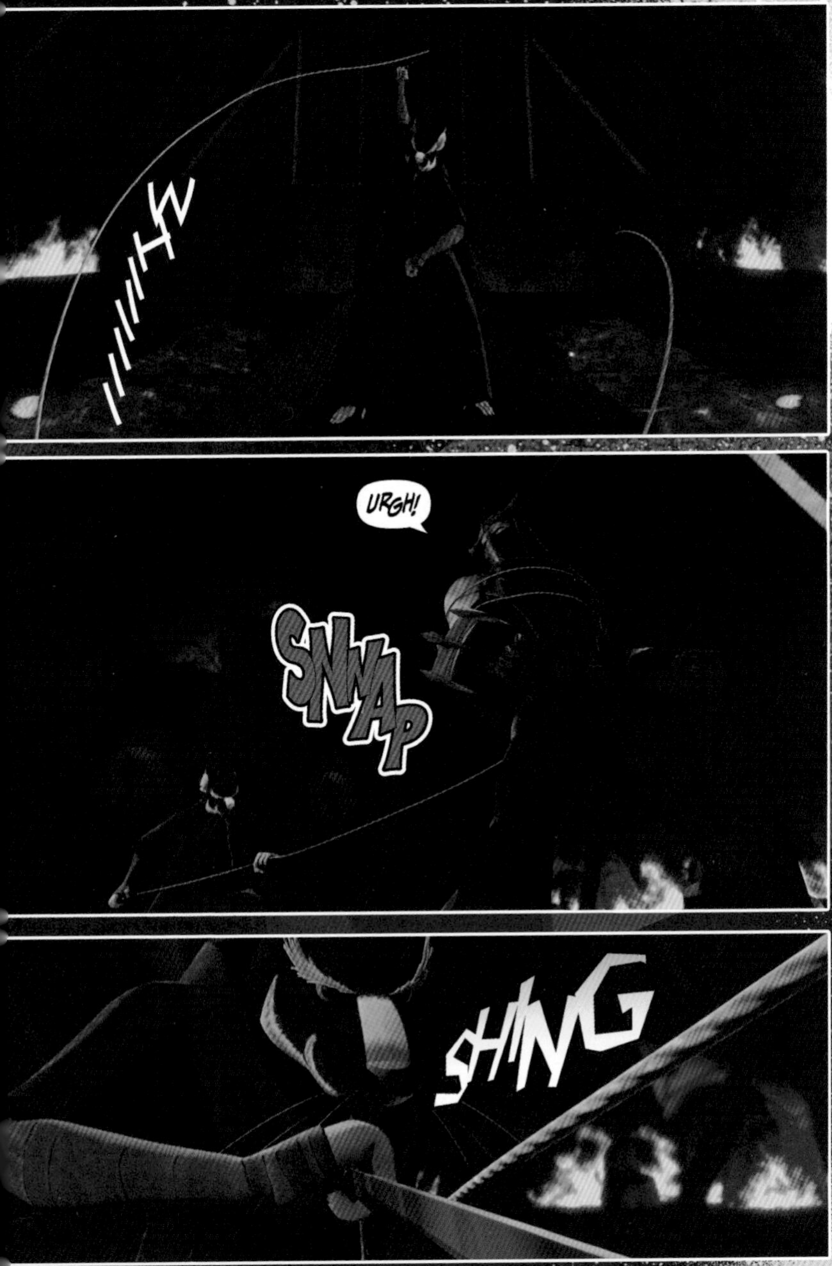
WHHH
URGH!
SNNAP
SHING

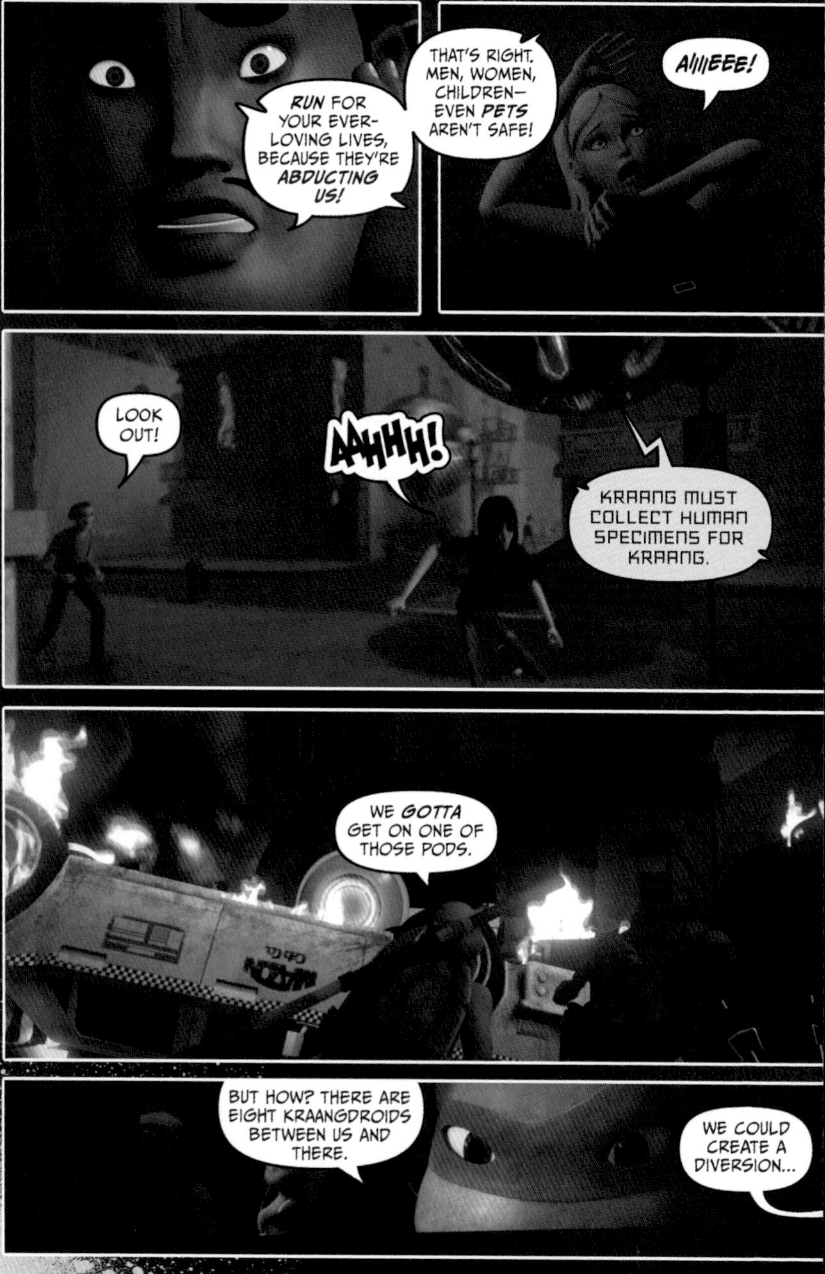

RUN FOR YOUR EVER-LOVING LIVES, BECAUSE THEY'RE ABDUCTING US!
THAT'S RIGHT. MEN, WOMEN, CHILDREN—EVEN PETS AREN'T SAFE!
AIIIIEEE!
LOOK OUT!
AAHHH!
KRAANG MUST COLLECT HUMAN SPECIMENS FOR KRAANG.
WE GOTTA GET ON ONE OF THOSE PODS.
BUT HOW? THERE ARE EIGHT KRAANGDROIDS BETWEEN US AND THERE.
WE COULD CREATE A DIVERSION...

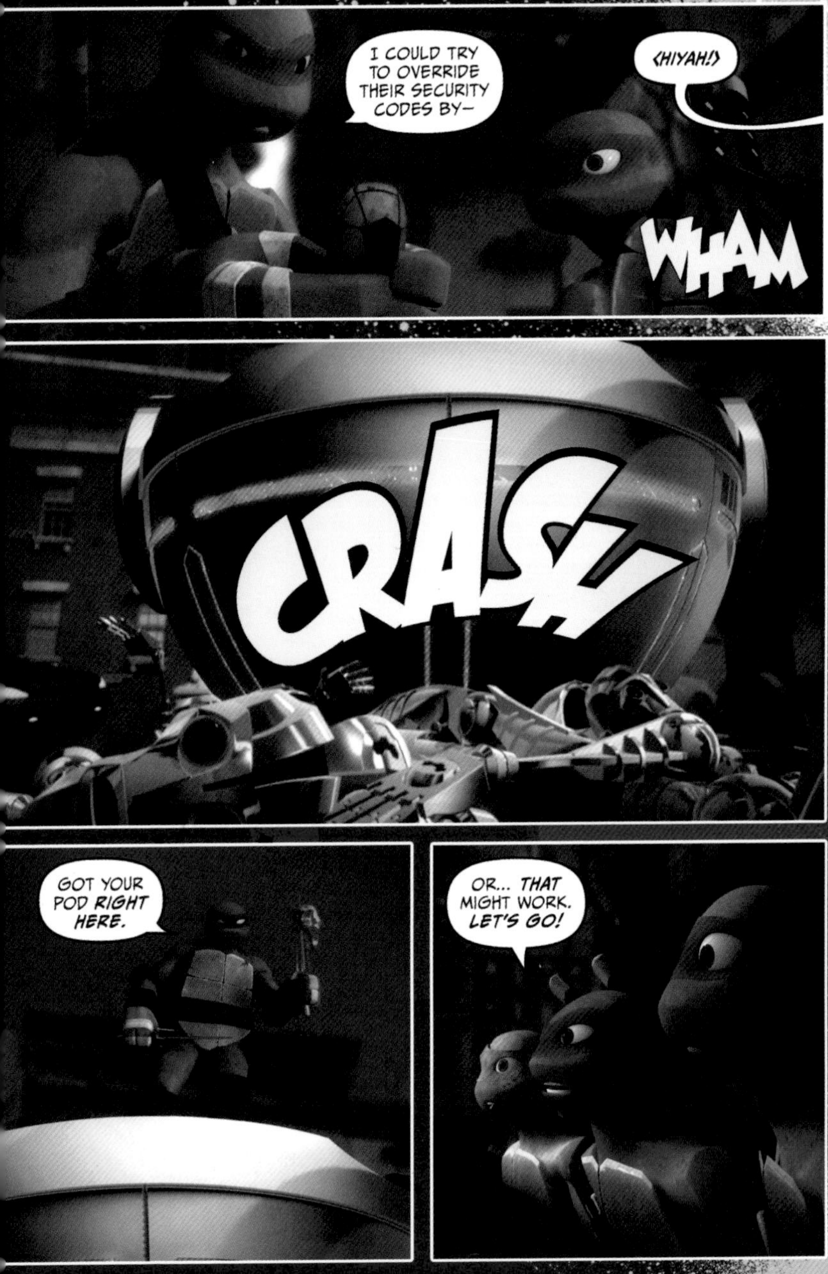
I COULD TRY TO OVERRIDE THEIR SECURITY CODES BY–
‹HIYAH!›
WHAM
CRASH
GOT YOUR POD RIGHT HERE.
OR... THAT MIGHT WORK. LET'S GO!

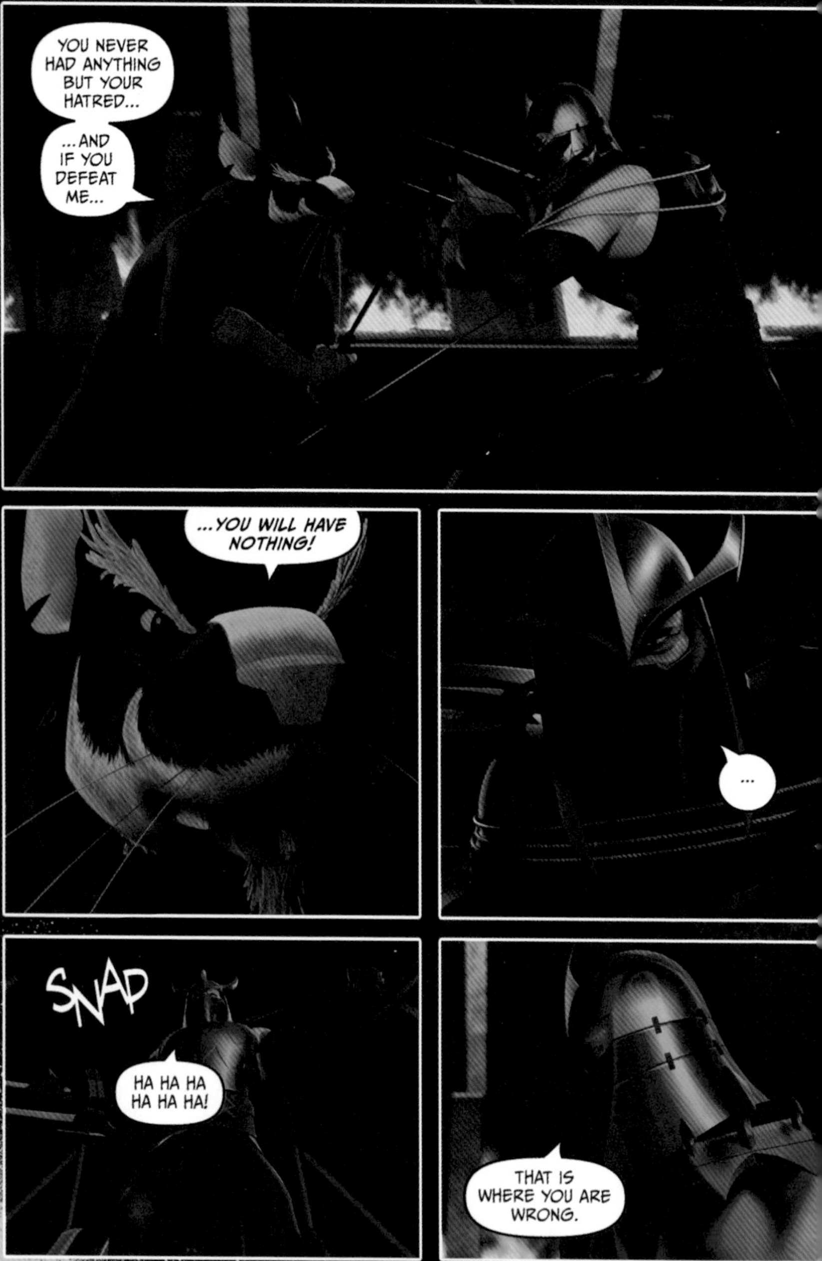
YOU NEVER HAD ANYTHING BUT YOUR HATRED...
...AND IF YOU DEFEAT ME...
...YOU WILL HAVE NOTHING!
...
SNAP
HA HA HA HA HA HA!
THAT IS WHERE YOU ARE WRONG.

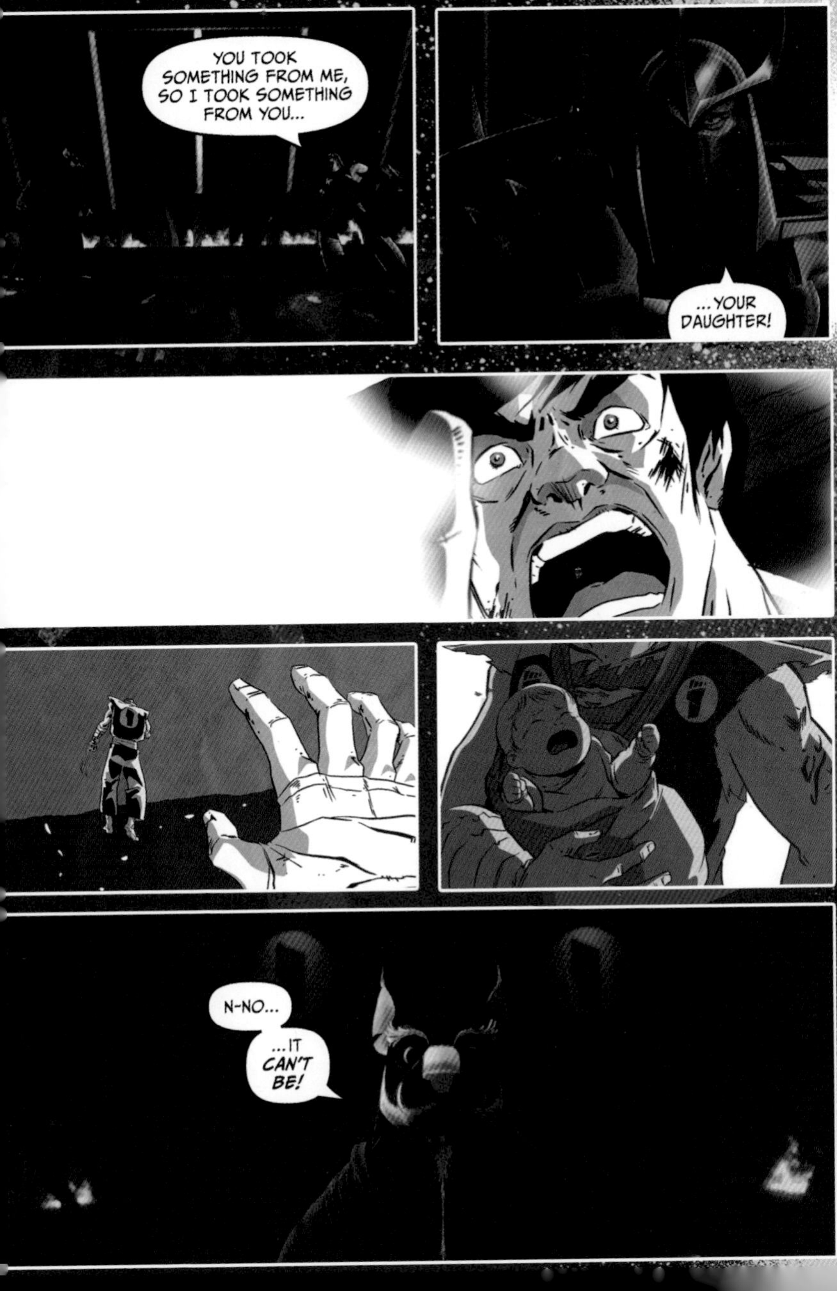

YOU TOOK SOMETHING FROM ME, SO I TOOK SOMETHING FROM YOU...
...YOUR DAUGHTER!
N-NO...
...IT CAN'T BE!

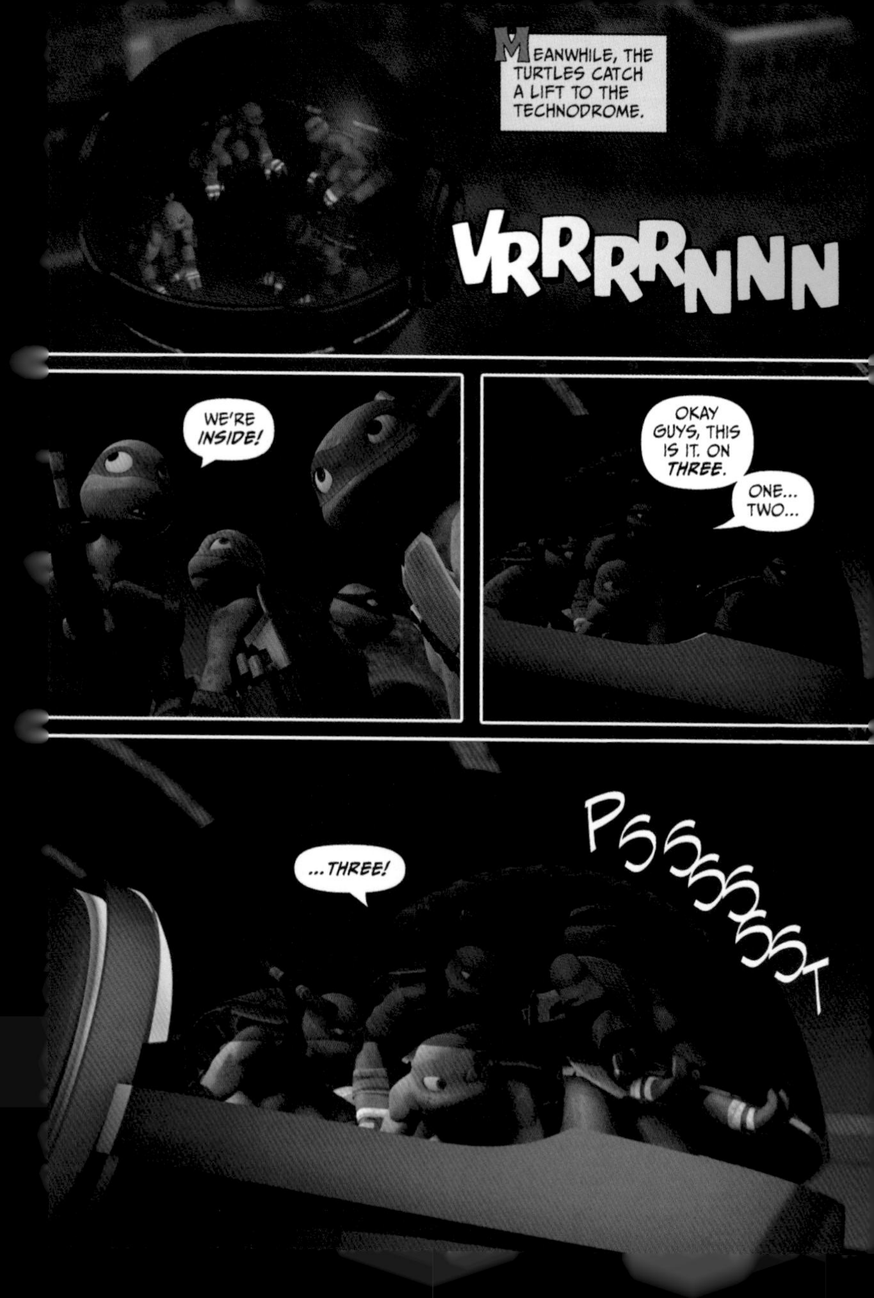
MEANWHILE, THE TURTLES CATCH A LIFT TO THE TECHNODROME.
VRRRRNNN
WE'RE INSIDE!
OKAY GUYS, THIS IS IT. ON THREE.
ONE... TWO...
...THREE!
PSSSSSSK

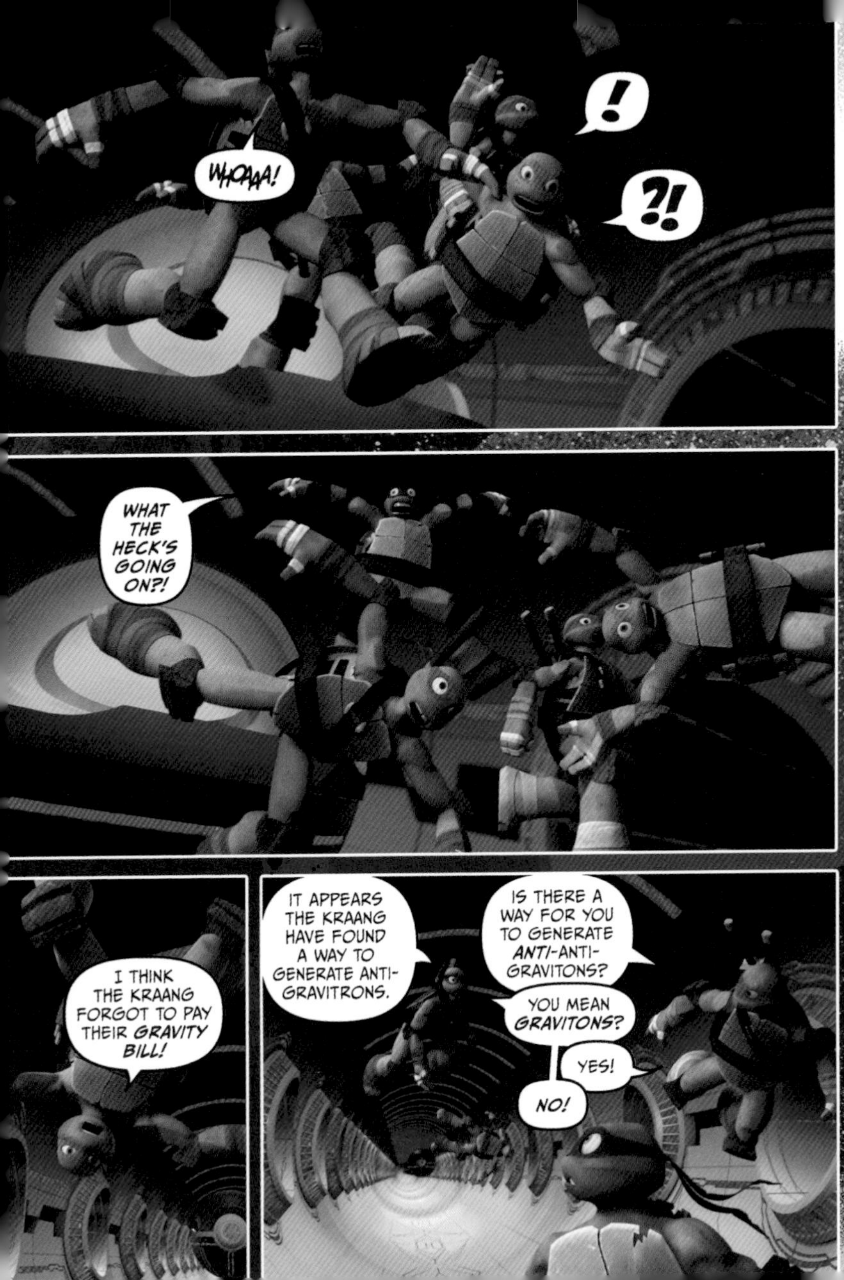
WHOAAA!
!
?!
WHAT THE HECK'S GOING ON?!
I THINK THE KRAANG FORGOT TO PAY THEIR GRAVITY BILL!
IT APPEARS THE KRAANG HAVE FOUND A WAY TO GENERATE ANTI-GRAVITRONS.
IS THERE A WAY FOR YOU TO GENERATE ANTI-ANTI-GRAVITONS?
YOU MEAN GRAVITONS?
YES!
NO!

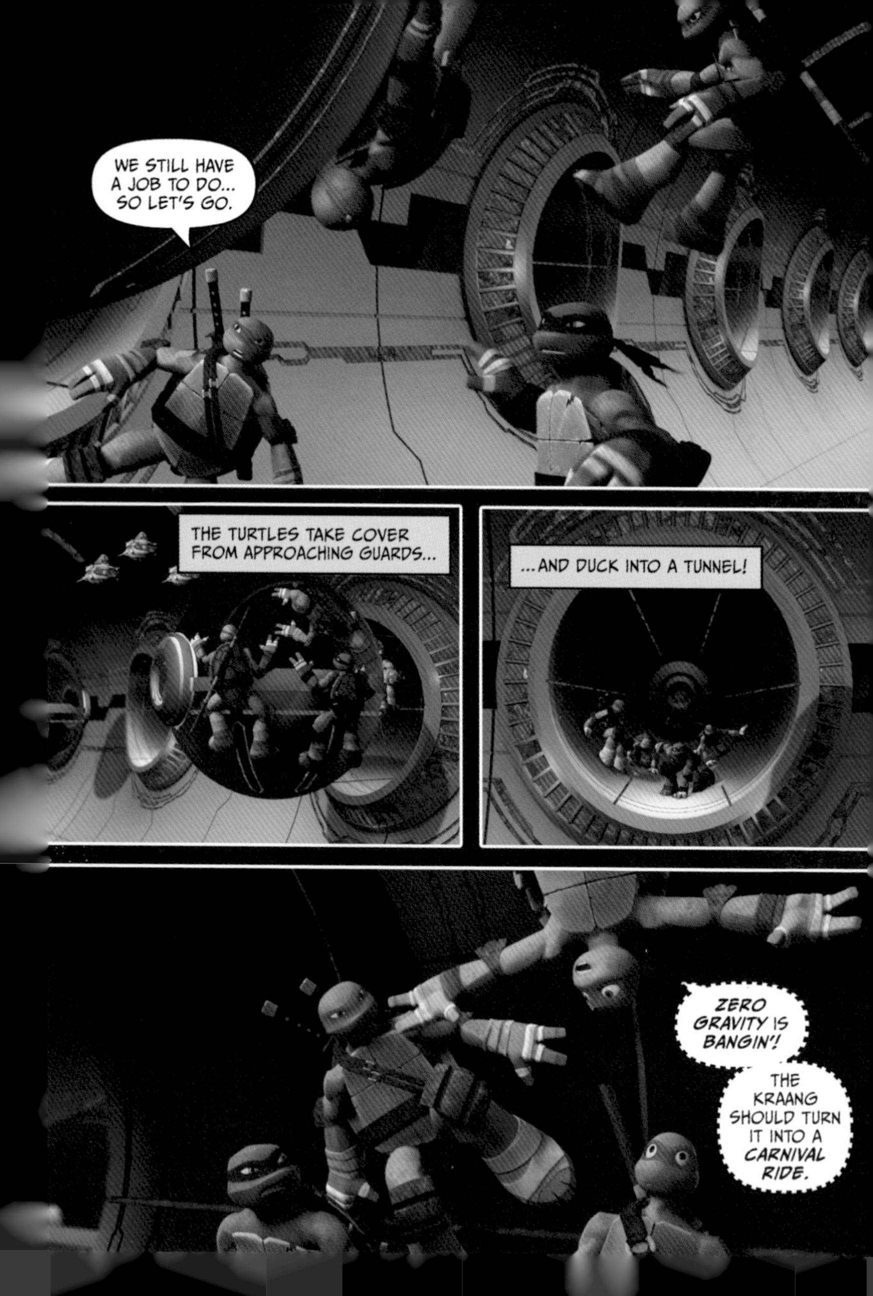
WE STILL HAVE A JOB TO DO... SO LET'S GO.
THE TURTLES TAKE COVER FROM APPROACHING GUARDS...
...AND DUCK INTO A TUNNEL!
ZERO GRAVITY IS BANGIN'!
THE KRAANG SHOULD TURN IT INTO A CARNIVAL RIDE.

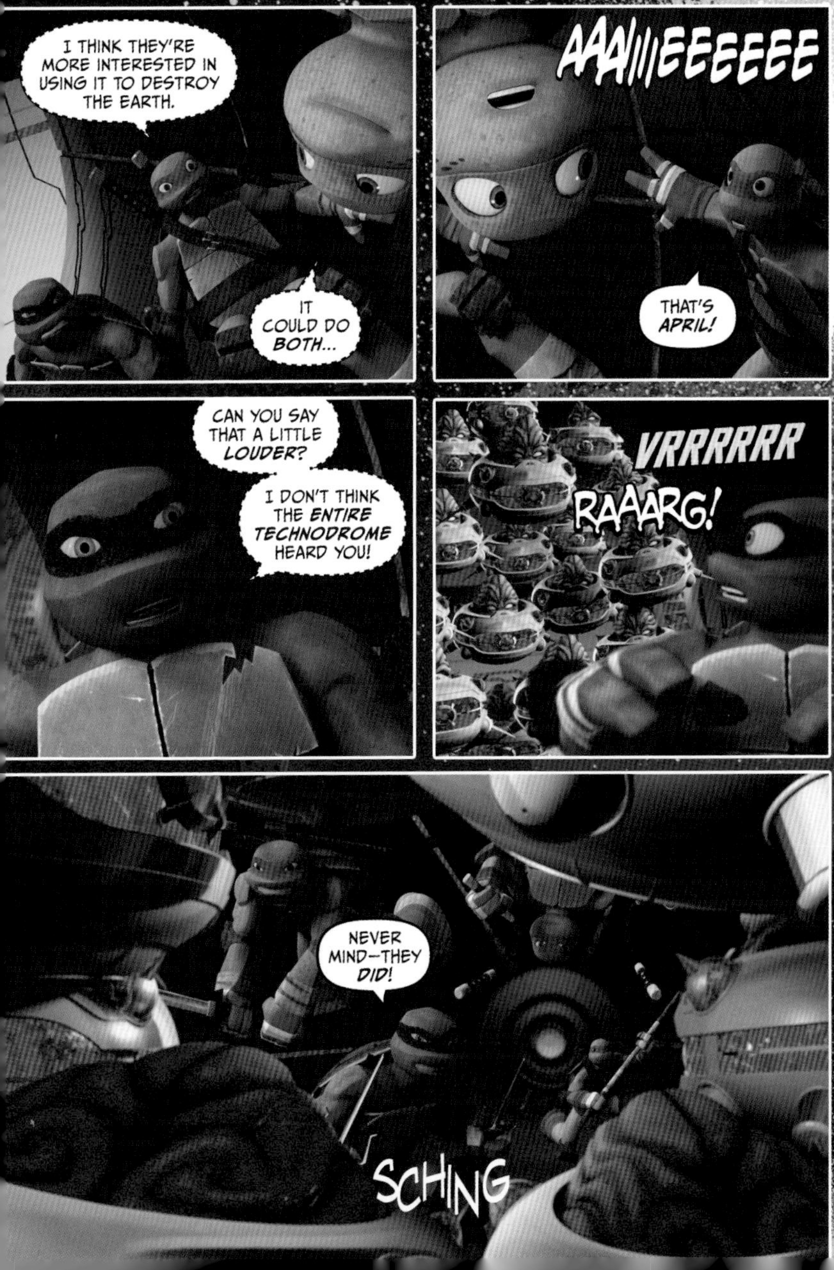
I THINK THEY'RE MORE INTERESTED IN USING IT TO DESTROY THE EARTH.
IT COULD DO *BOTH*...
AAAIIIIIEEEEEE
THAT'S *APRIL!*
CAN YOU SAY THAT A LITTLE *LOUDER?*
I DON'T THINK THE *ENTIRE TECHNODROME* HEARD YOU!
VRRRRRR
RAAARG!
NEVER MIND—THEY *DID!*
SCHING

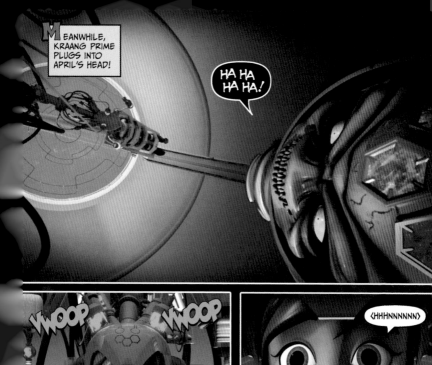

MEANWHILE, KRAANG PRIME PLUGS INTO APRIL'S HEAD!

HA HA HA HA!

VWOOP VWOOP

〈HHHNNNNNN〉

〈HHHNNNNNN〉

YES... YES!

IT'S WORKING!

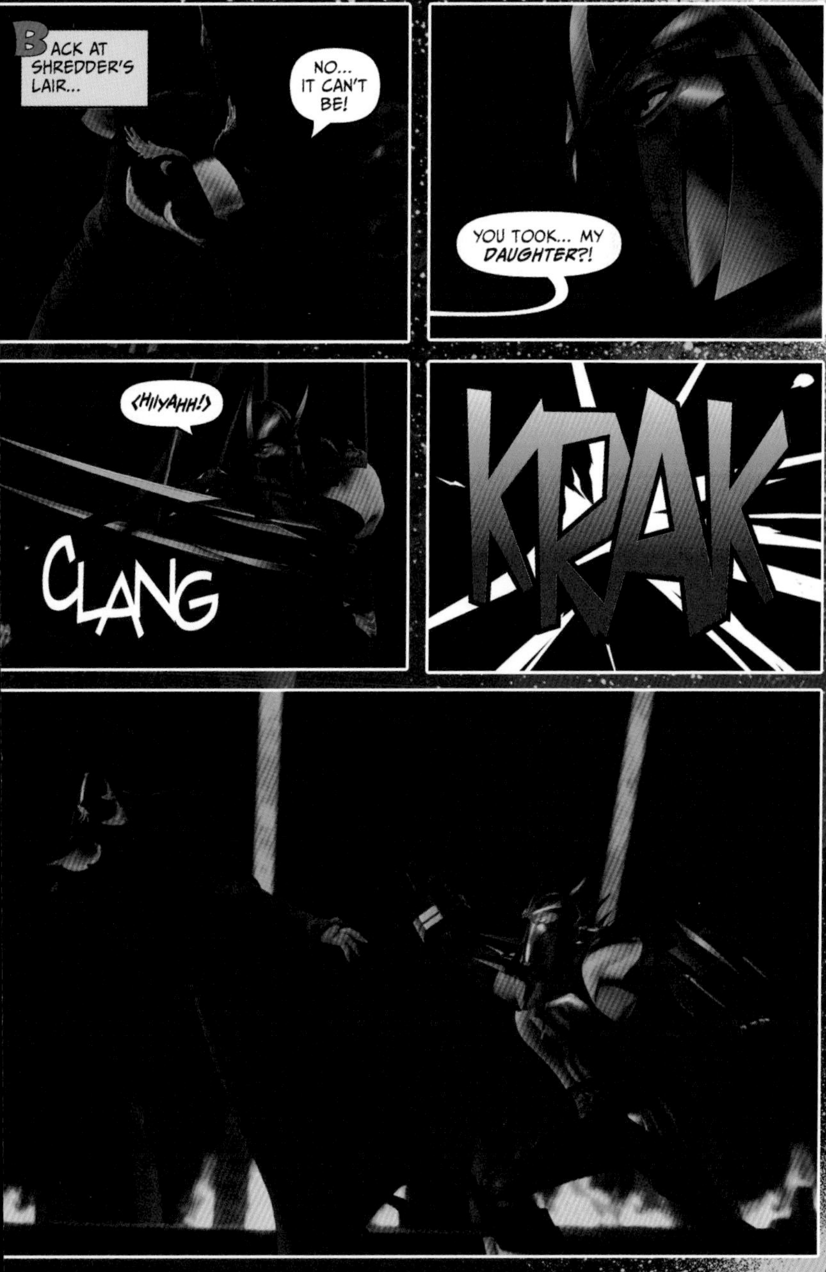
BACK AT SHREDDER'S LAIR...
NO... IT CAN'T BE!
YOU TOOK... MY DAUGHTER?!
<HIIYAHH!>
CLANG
KRAK

IT'S *OVER*, HAMATO.

SOON YOU WILL BE NO MORE, AND YOUR OWN DAUGHTER WILL GO THROUGH HER LIFE *CURSING* YOUR NAME!

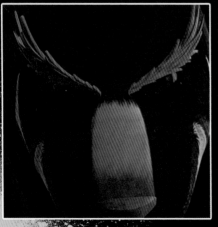

WOOOOOSH

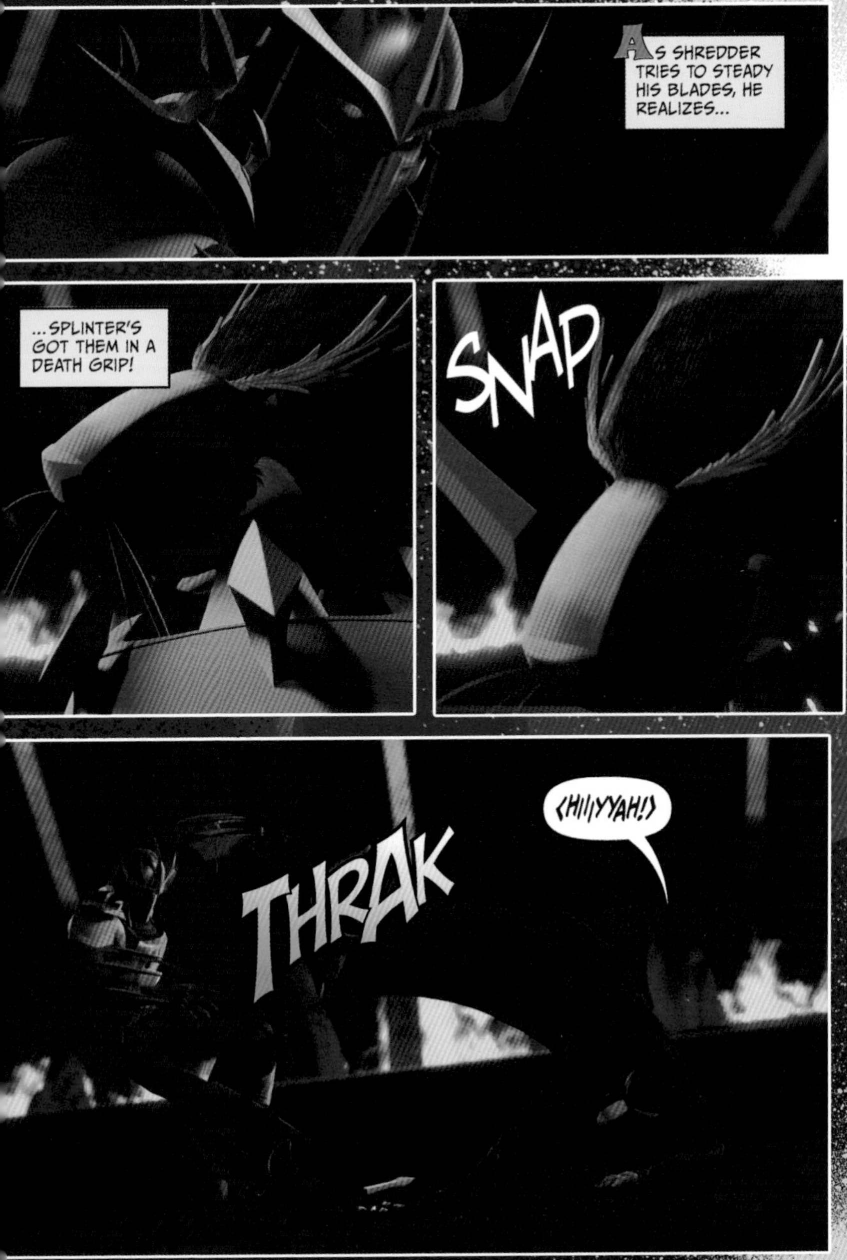
AS SHREDDER TRIES TO STEADY HIS BLADES, HE REALIZES...
...SPLINTER'S GOT THEM IN A DEATH GRIP!
SNAP
‹HIIIYYAH!›
THRAK

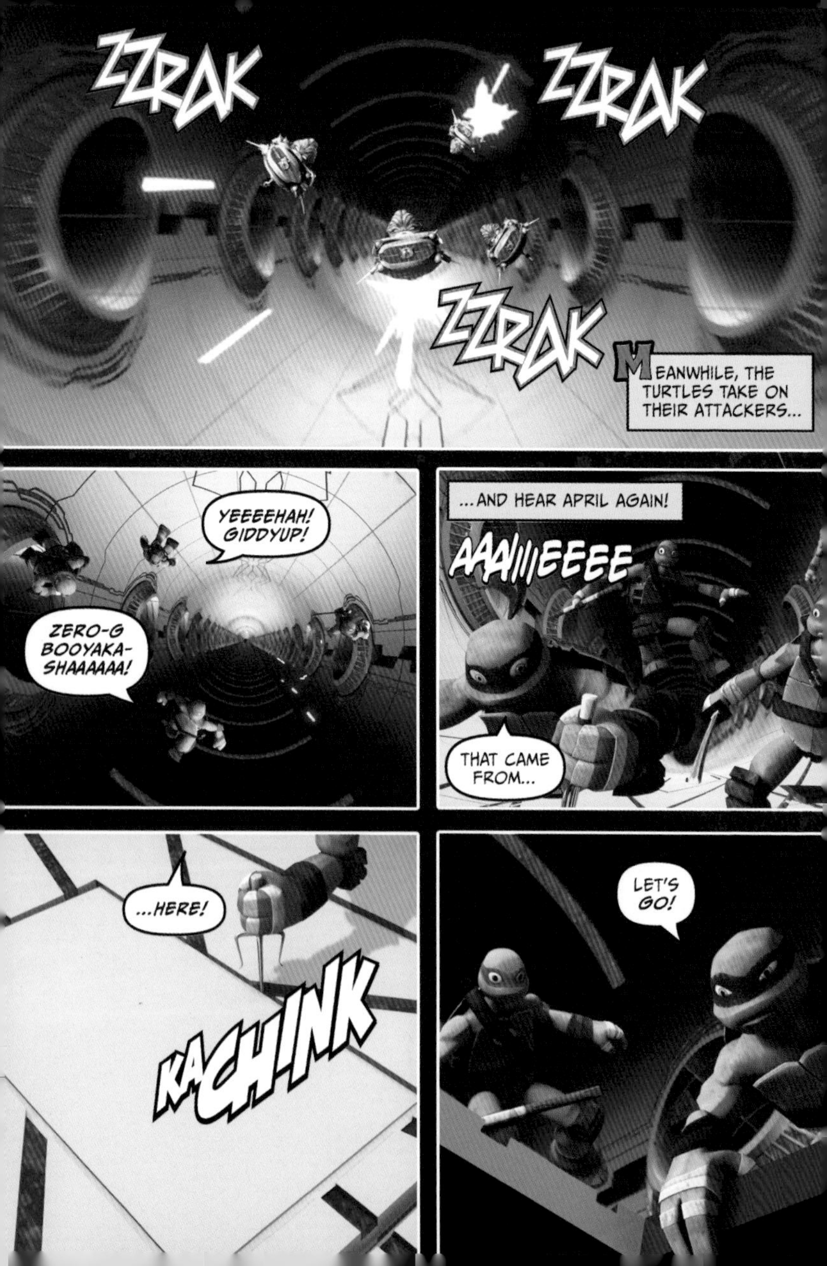
ZZRAK
ZZRAK
ZZRAK
MEANWHILE, THE TURTLES TAKE ON THEIR ATTACKERS...
YEEEEHAH! GIDDYUP!
ZERO-G BOOYAKA-SHAAAAAA!
...AND HEAR APRIL AGAIN!
AAAIIIIEEEE
THAT CAME FROM...
...HERE!
KACHINK
LET'S GO!

APRIL O'NEIL...

...YOUR MIND BELONGS TO KRAANG!

SOON YOUR WORLD WILL BE OURS!

LET THE PLANETARY MUTATION BEGIN!

WITNESS THE END OF YOUR KIND!

NOT IF WE CAN HELP IT!

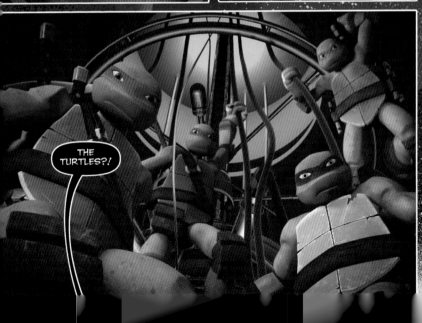

THE TURTLES?!

KRAANG WILL NOT BE STOPPED BY PATHETIC MUTANTS!

AT LEAST WE'RE NOT STUPID ALIENS!

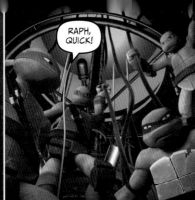

RAPH, QUICK!

ON IT!

WHAM

RAAAAARRRG!

WE'RE HERE, APRIL.

AS DONNIE FREES APRIL FROM THE MACHINE...

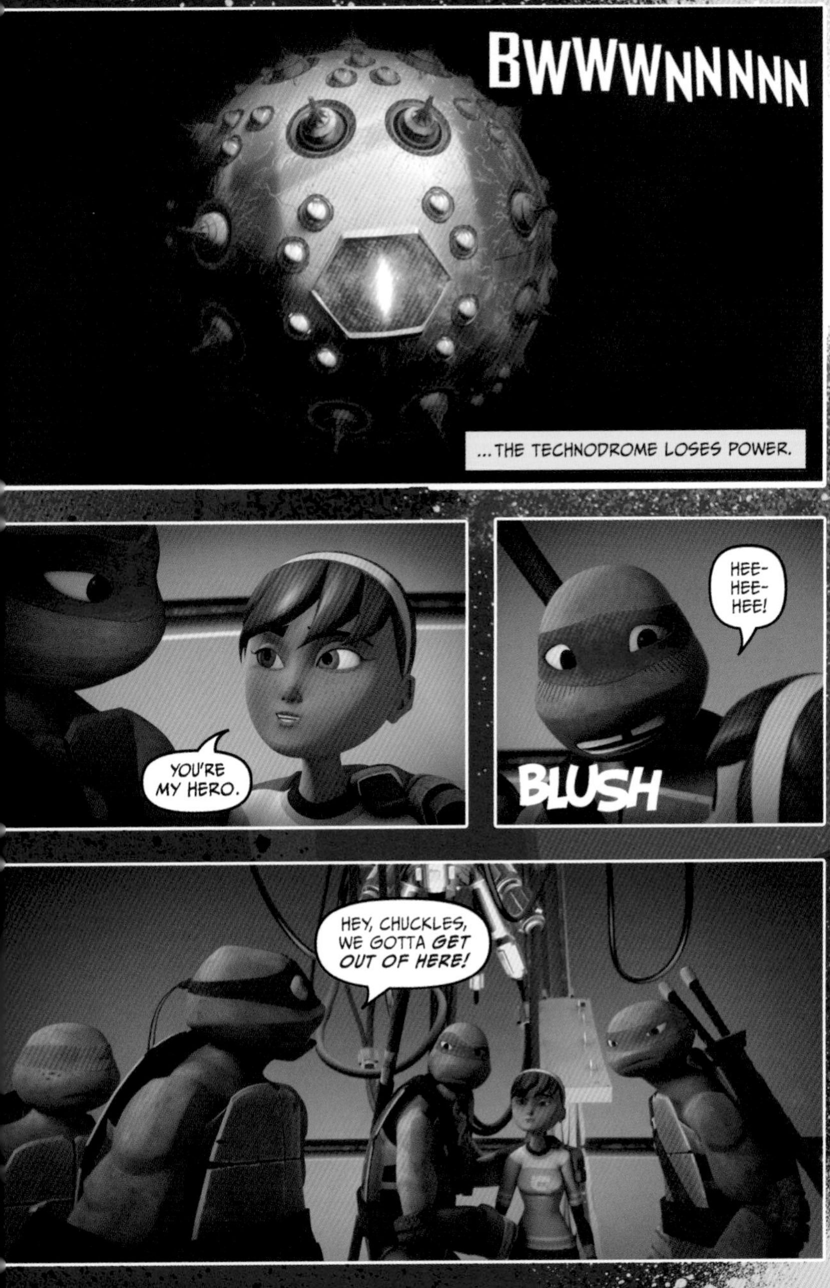
BWWWNNNNN
...THE TECHNODROME LOSES POWER.
YOU'RE MY HERO.
HEE-HEE-HEE!
BLUSH
HEY, CHUCKLES, WE GOTTA GET OUT OF HERE!

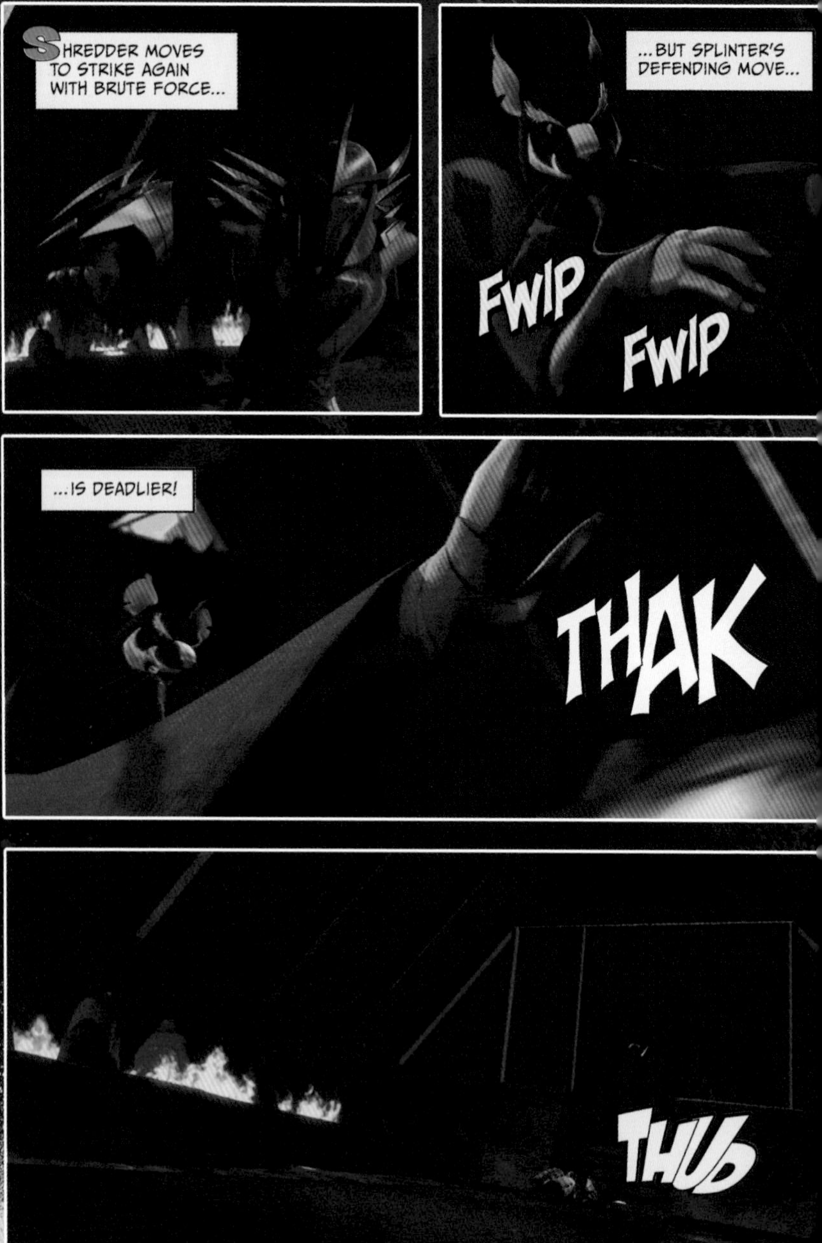
SHREDDER MOVES TO STRIKE AGAIN WITH BRUTE FORCE...
...BUT SPLINTER'S DEFENDING MOVE...
FWIP
FWIP
...IS DEADLIER!
THAK
THUD

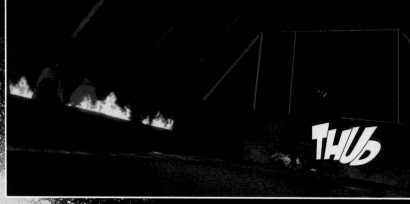

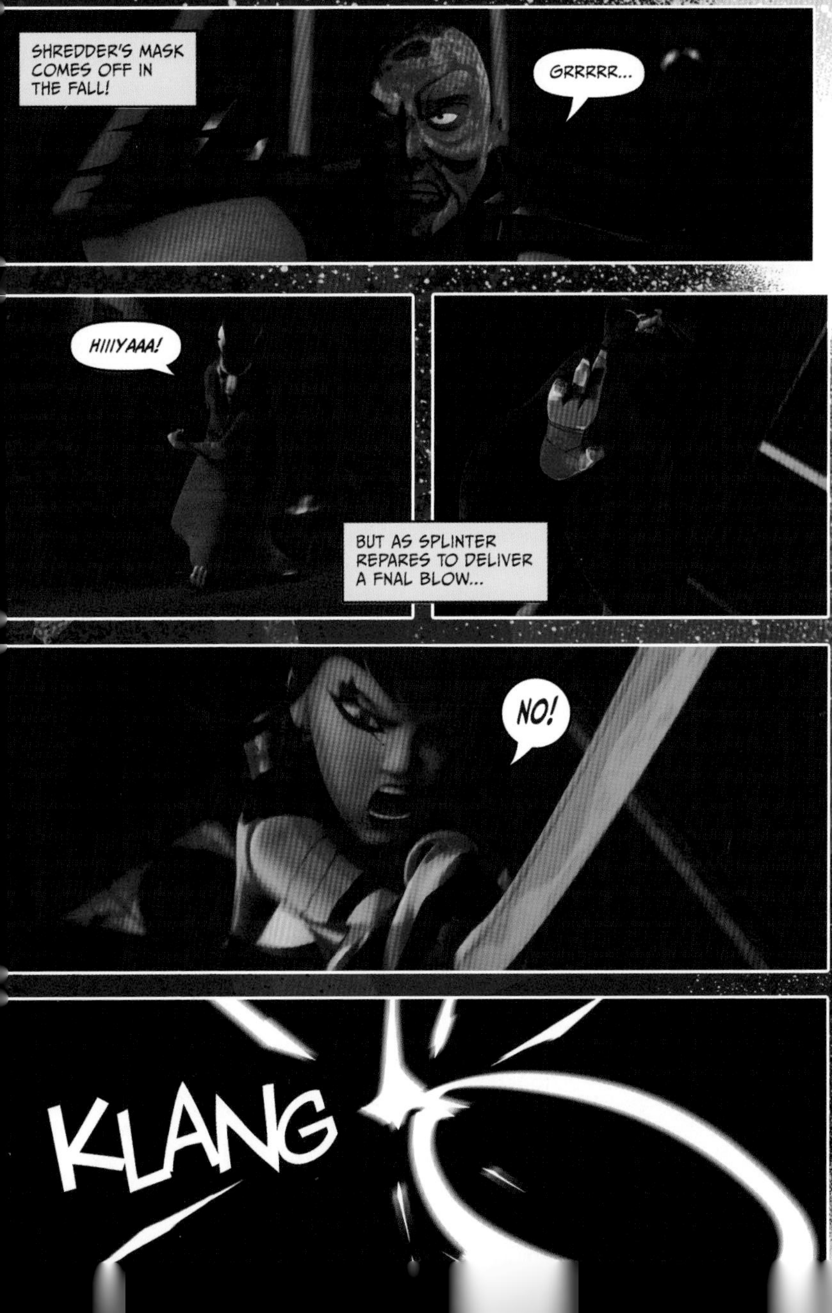
SHREDDER'S MASK COMES OFF IN THE FALL!
GRRRRR...
HIIIYAAA!
BUT AS SPLINTER REPARES TO DELIVER A FNAL BLOW...
NO!
KLANG

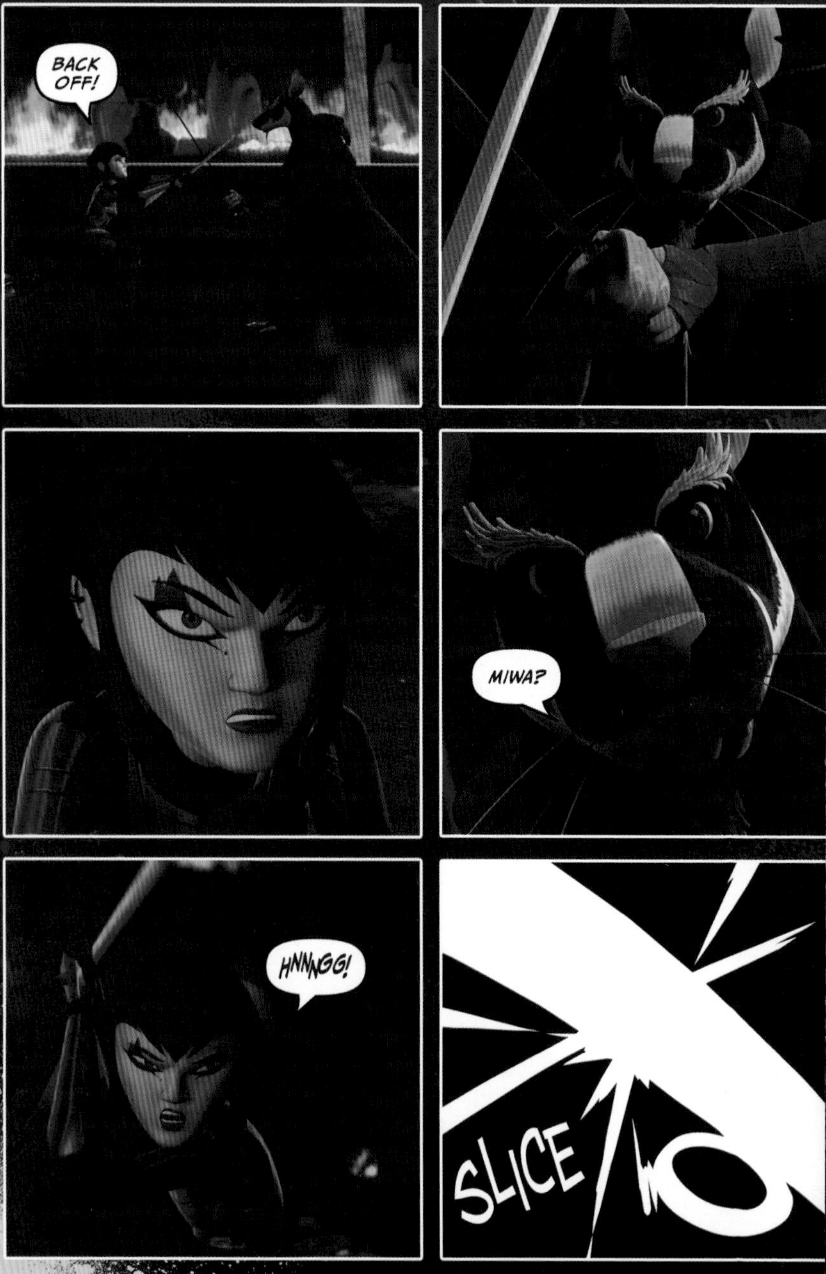
BACK OFF!
MIWA?
HNNNGG!
SLICE

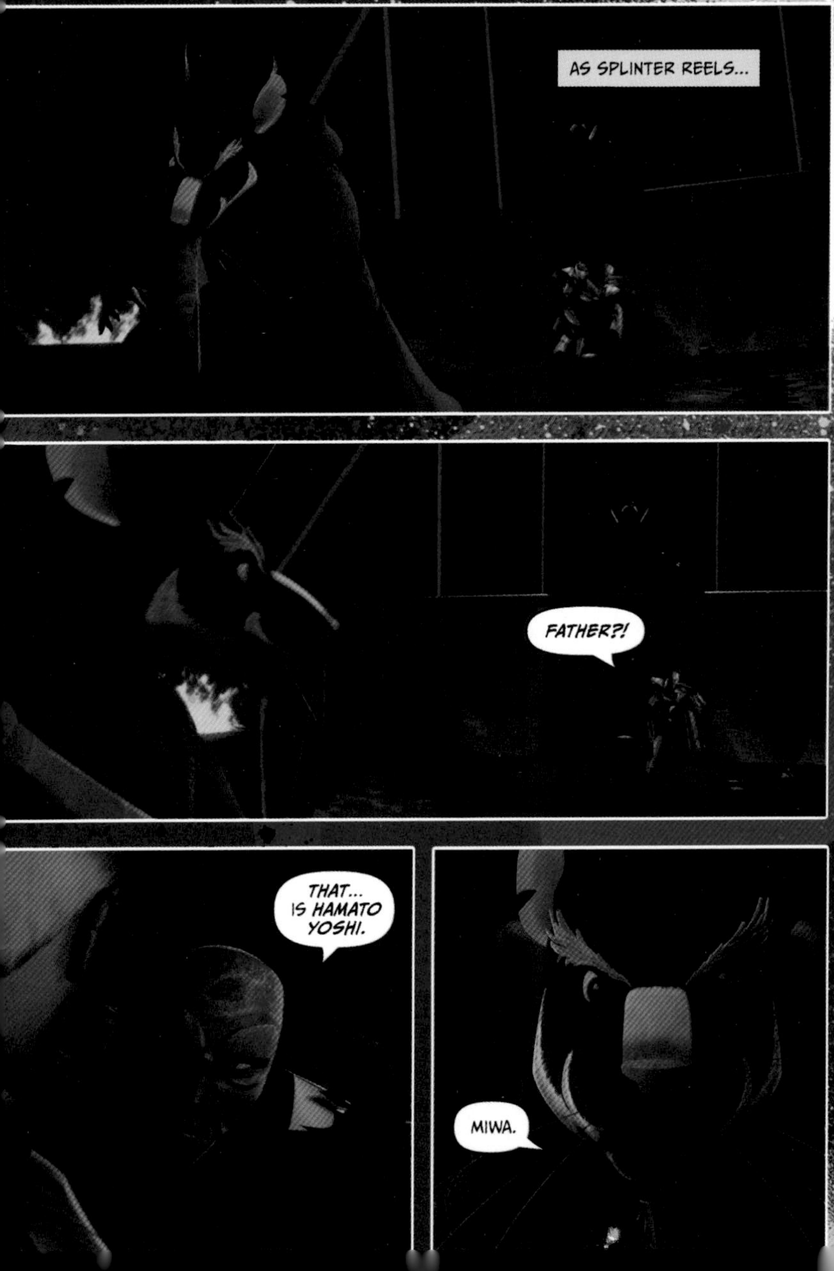
AS SPLINTER REELS...
FATHER?!
THAT... IS HAMATO YOSHI.
MIWA.

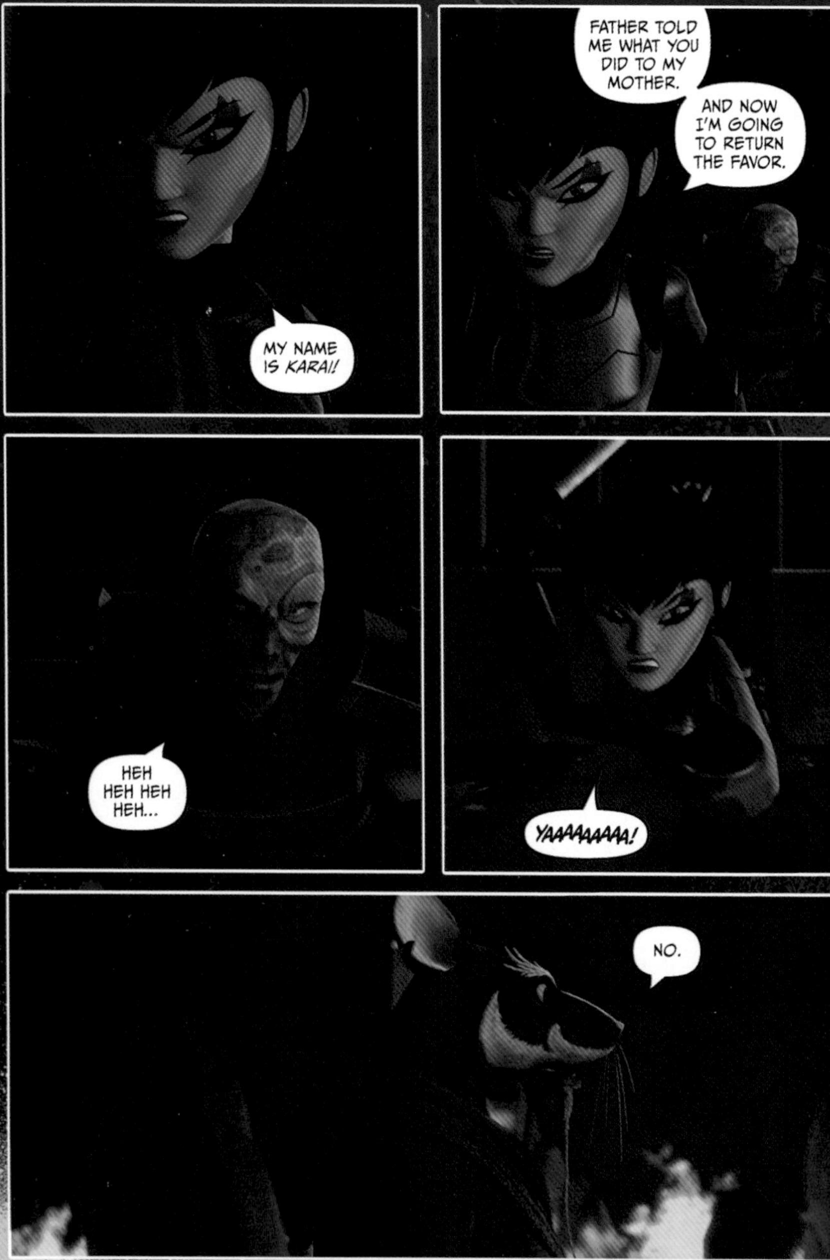
MY NAME IS KARAI!
FATHER TOLD ME WHAT YOU DID TO MY MOTHER.
AND NOW I'M GOING TO RETURN THE FAVOR.
HEH HEH HEH HEH...
YAAAAAAAAA!
NO.

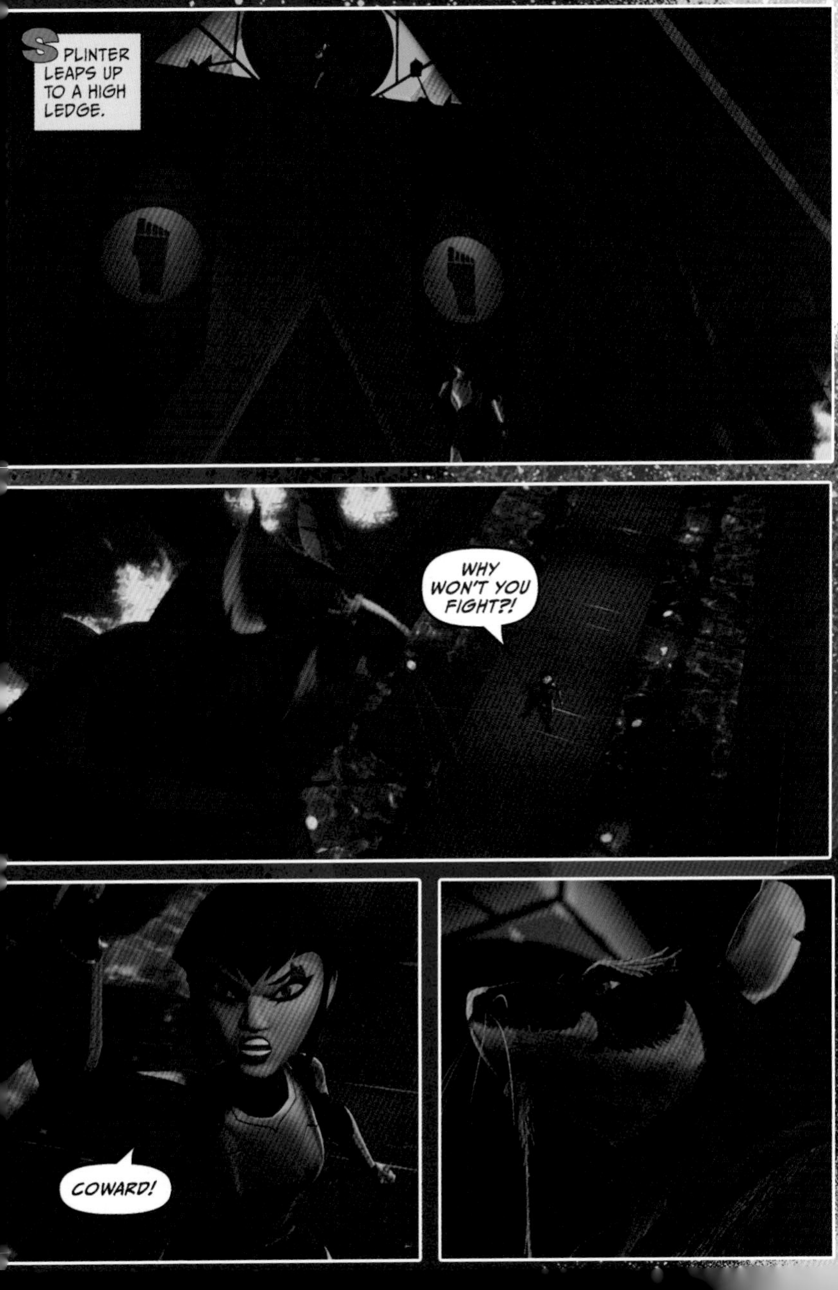
SPLINTER LEAPS UP TO A HIGH LEDGE.
WHY WON'T YOU FIGHT?!
COWARD!

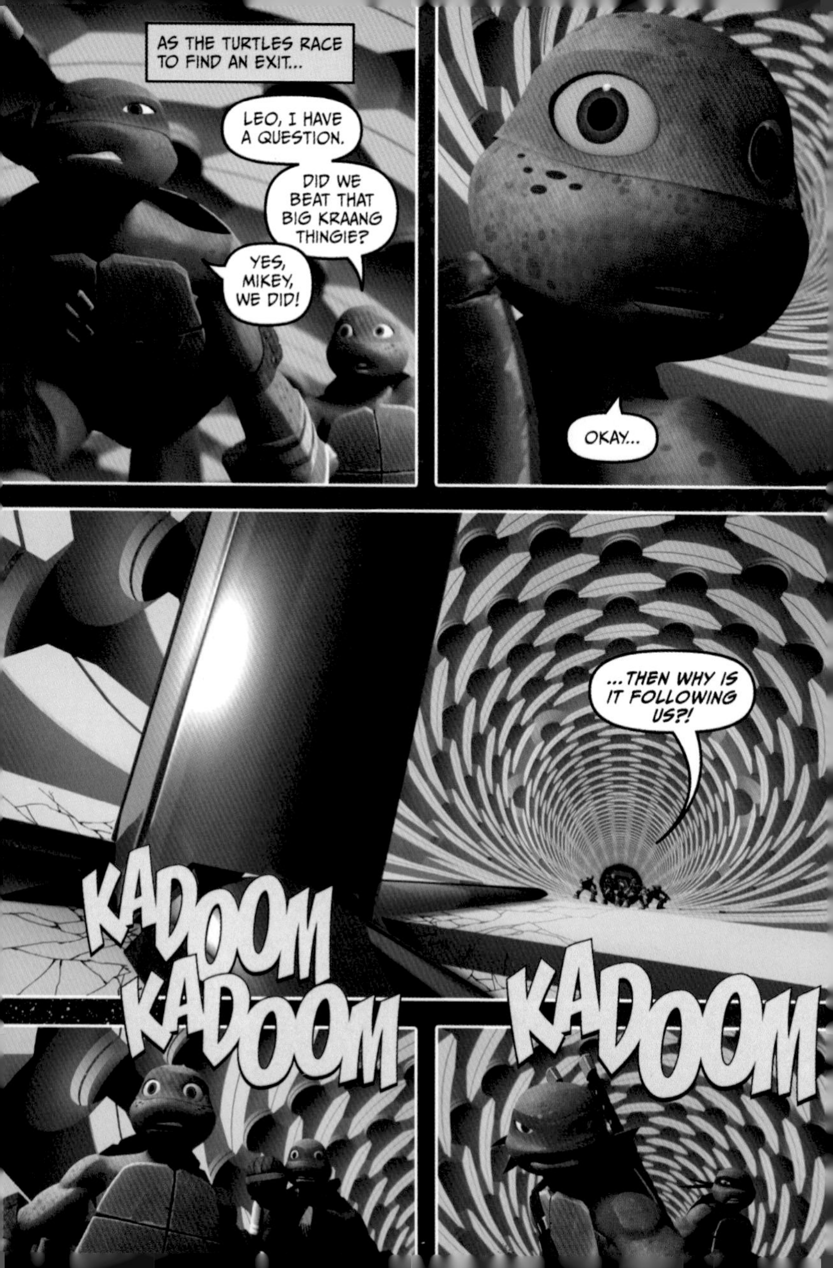
AS THE TURTLES RACE TO FIND AN EXIT...
LEO, I HAVE A QUESTION.
DID WE BEAT THAT BIG KRAANG THINGIE?
YES, MIKEY, WE DID!
OKAY...
...THEN WHY IS IT FOLLOWING US?!
KADOOM
KADOOM
KADOOM

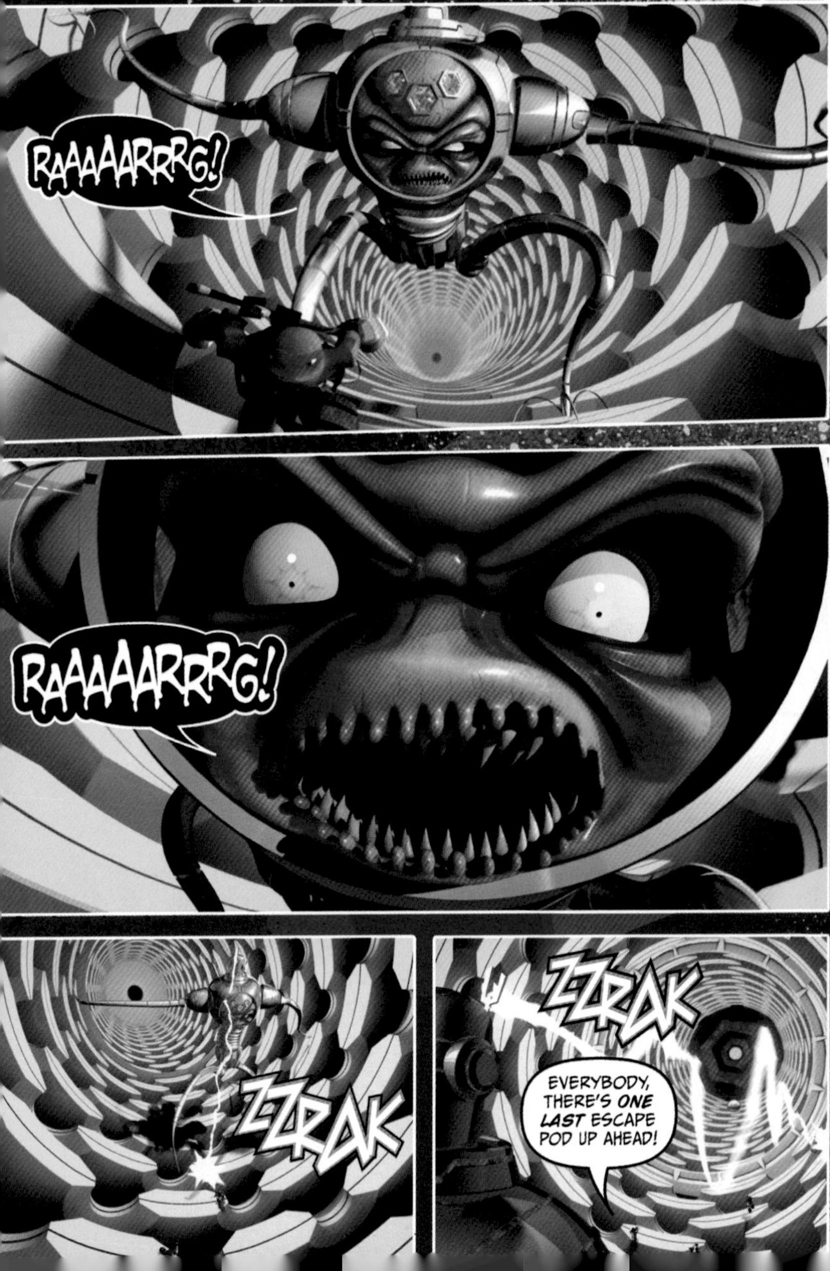
RAAAAARRRG!
RAAAAARRRG!
ZZRAK
ZZRAK
EVERYBODY, THERE'S *ONE LAST* ESCAPE POD UP AHEAD!

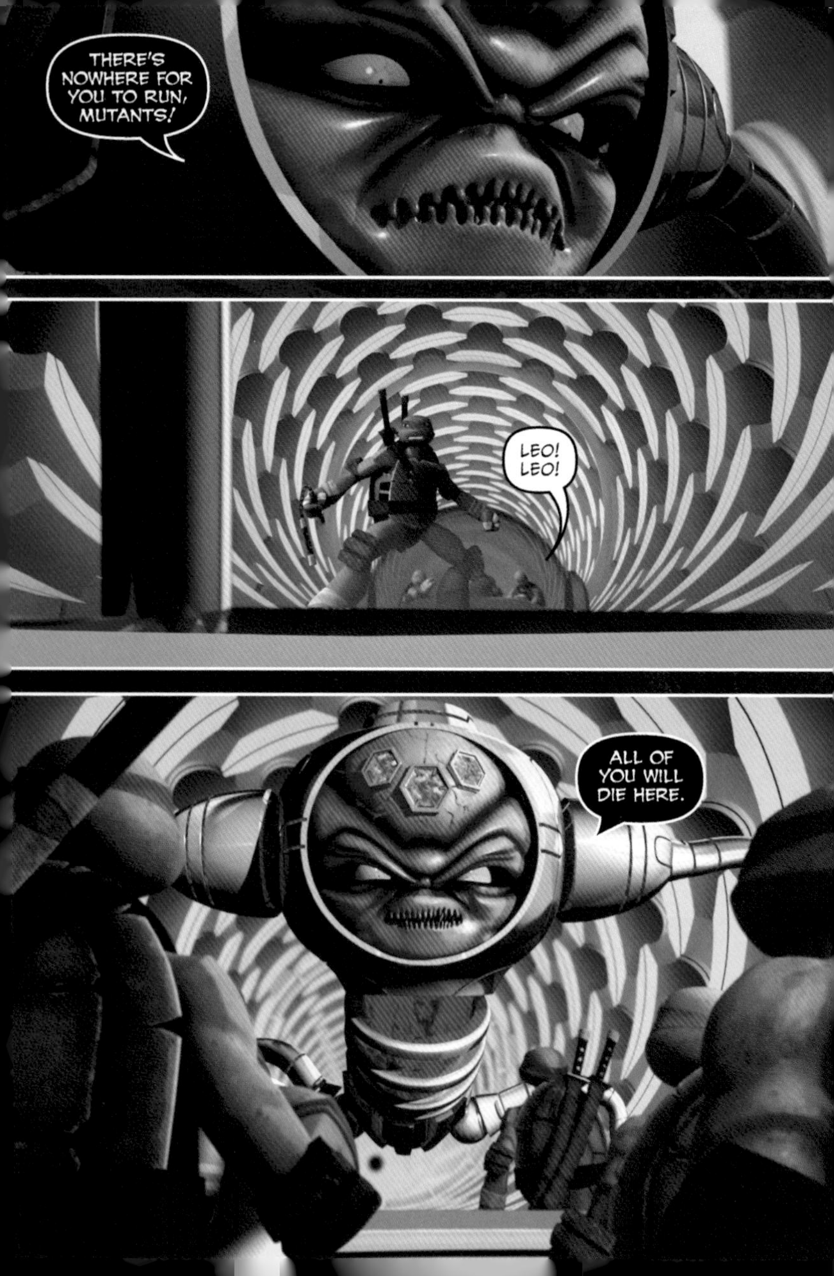
THERE'S NOWHERE FOR YOU TO RUN, MUTANTS!
LEO! LEO!
ALL OF YOU WILL DIE HERE.

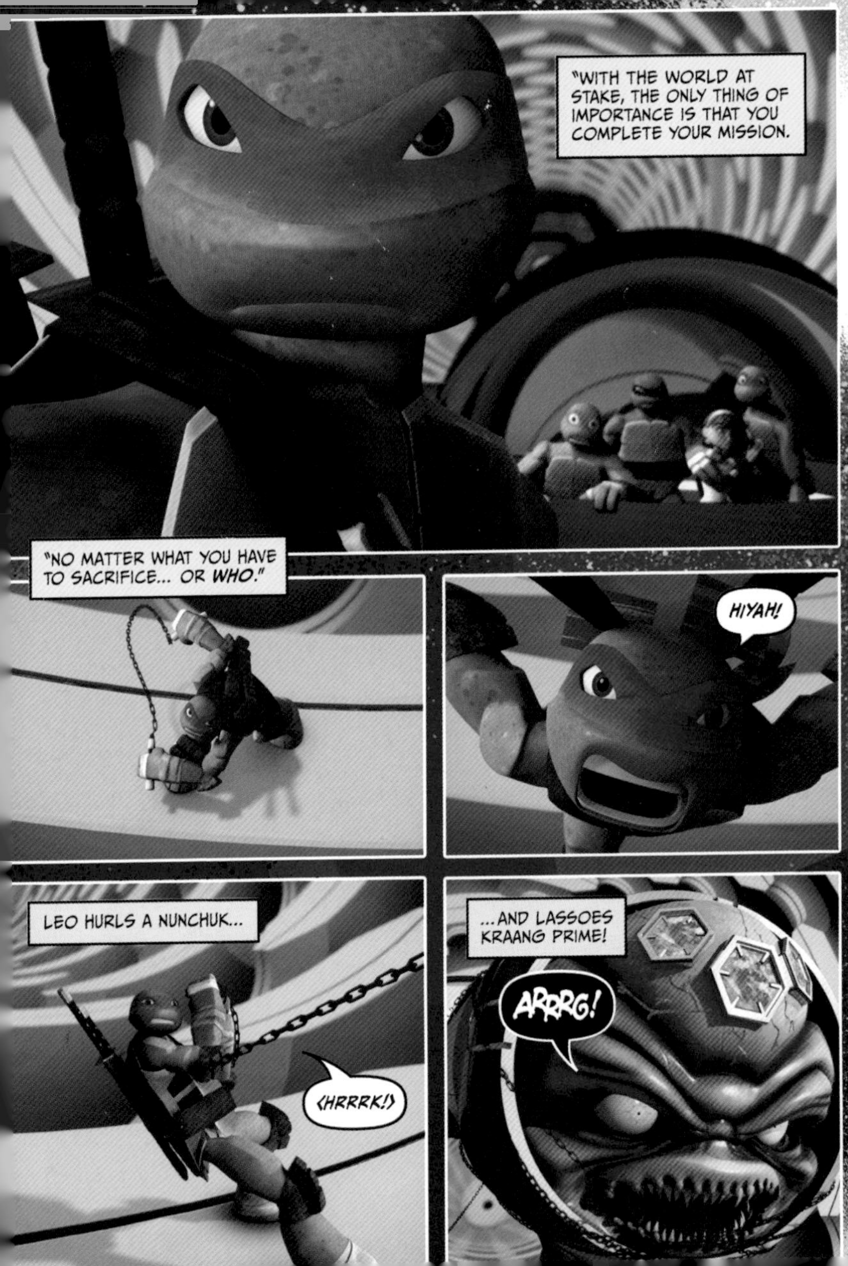
"WITH THE WORLD AT STAKE, THE ONLY THING OF IMPORTANCE IS THAT YOU COMPLETE YOUR MISSION.
"NO MATTER WHAT YOU HAVE TO SACRIFICE... OR *WHO.*"
HIYAH!
LEO HURLS A NUNCHUK...
<HRRRK!>
...AND LASSOES KRAANG PRIME!
ARRRG!

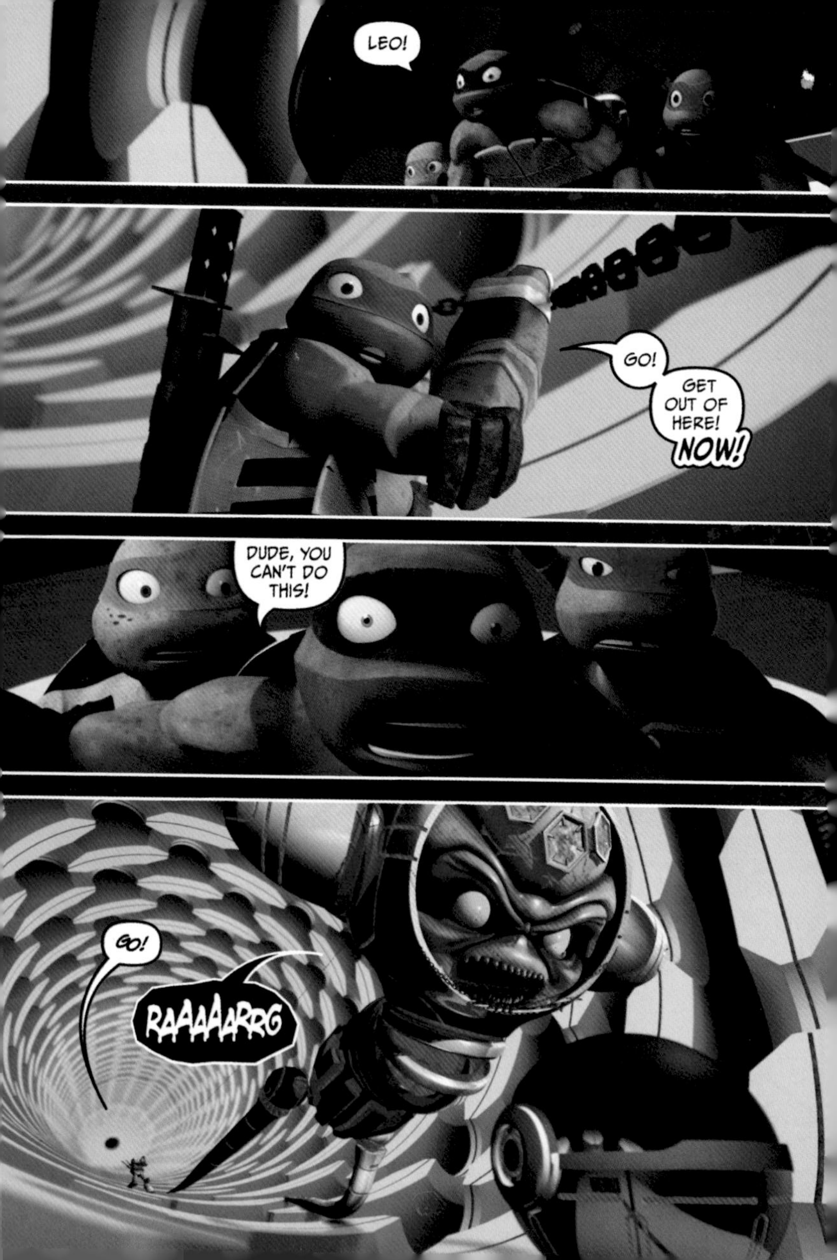
LEO!
GO!
GET OUT OF HERE! NOW!
DUDE, YOU CAN'T DO THIS!
GO!
RAAAAARRG

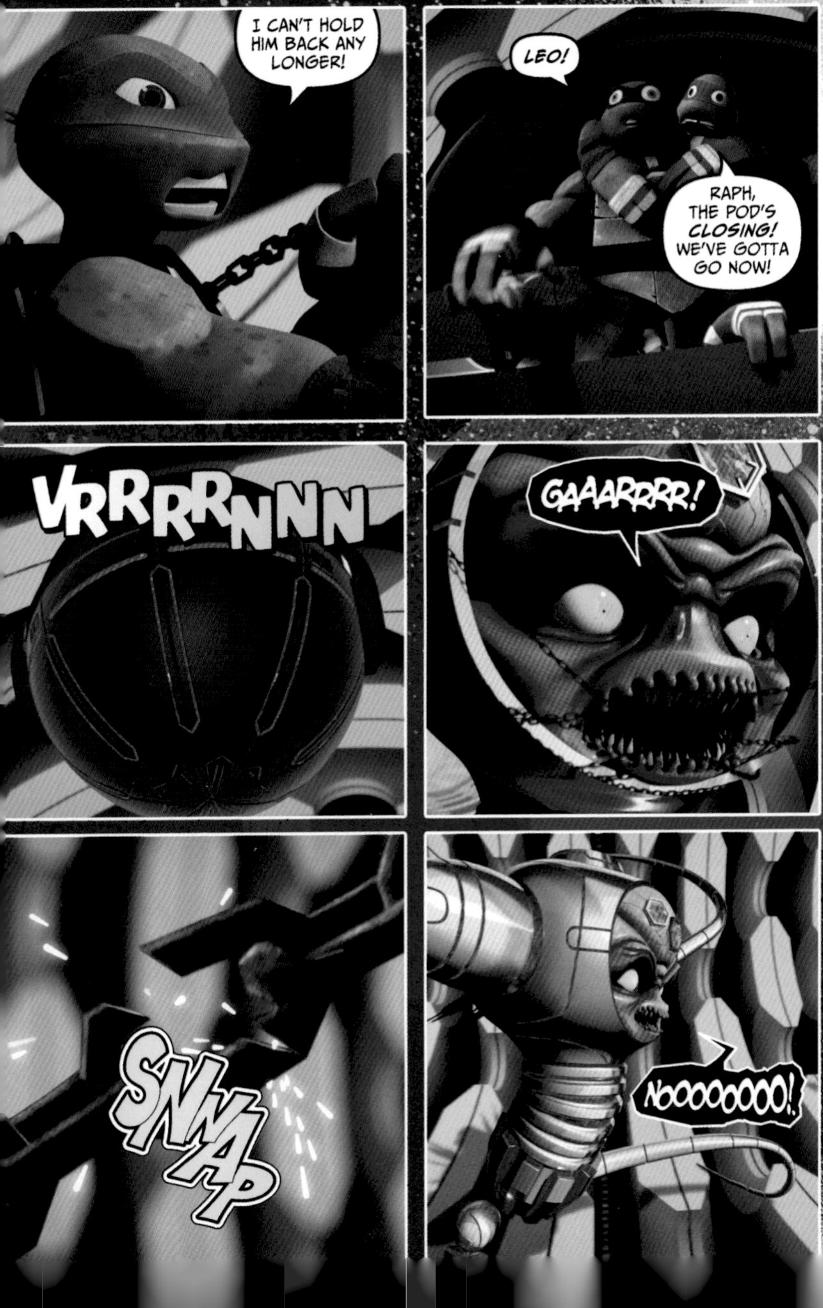
I CAN'T HOLD HIM BACK ANY LONGER!
LEO!
RAPH, THE POD'S *CLOSING!* WE'VE GOTTA GO NOW!
VRRRRNNN
GAAARRRR!
SNNAP
NOOOOOOO!

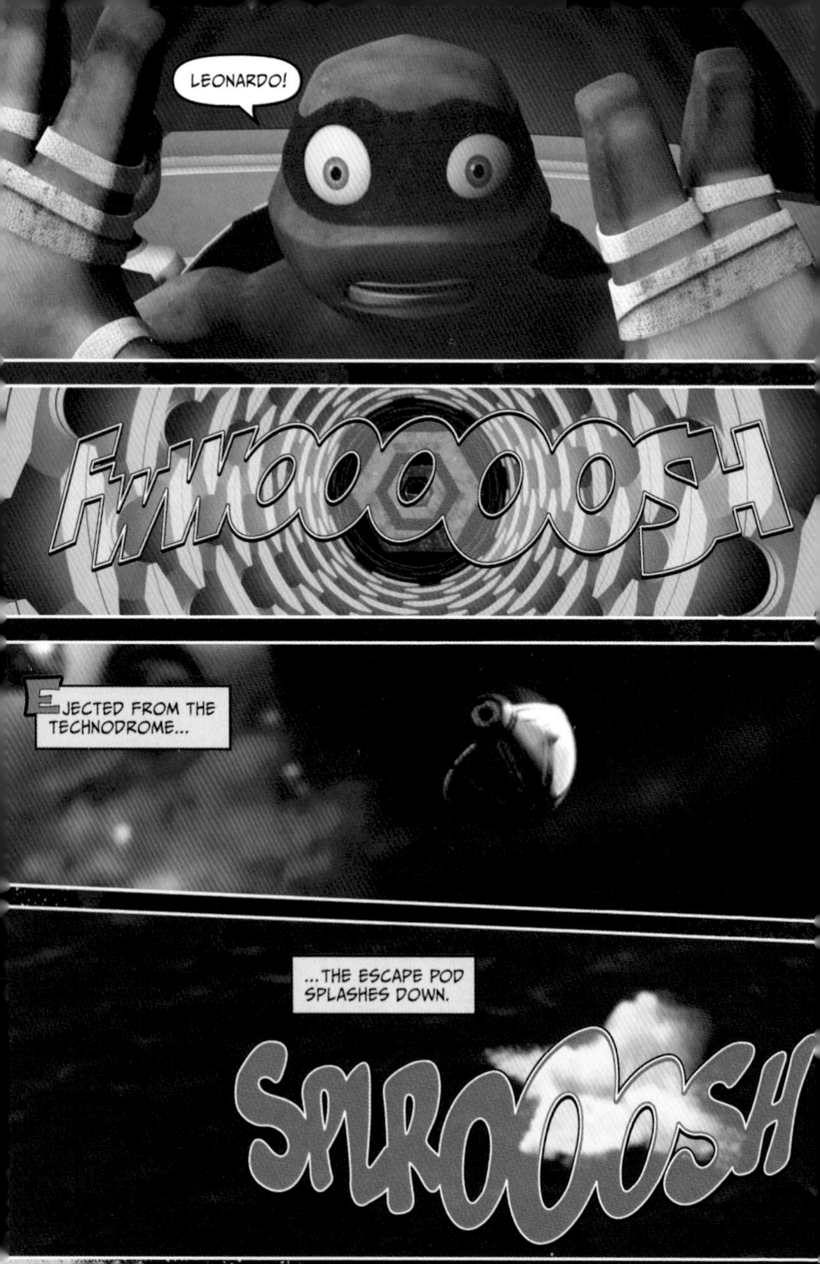
LEONARDO!
FWHOOOOOSH
EJECTED FROM THE TECHNODROME...
...THE ESCAPE POD SPLASHES DOWN.
SPLOOOOSH

I CAN'T BELIEVE IT. WE MADE IT.

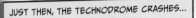
JUST THEN, THE TECHNODROME CRASHES...

PSSSSSH

FRROOMMM

LEO!

...AND SINKS.

NO!

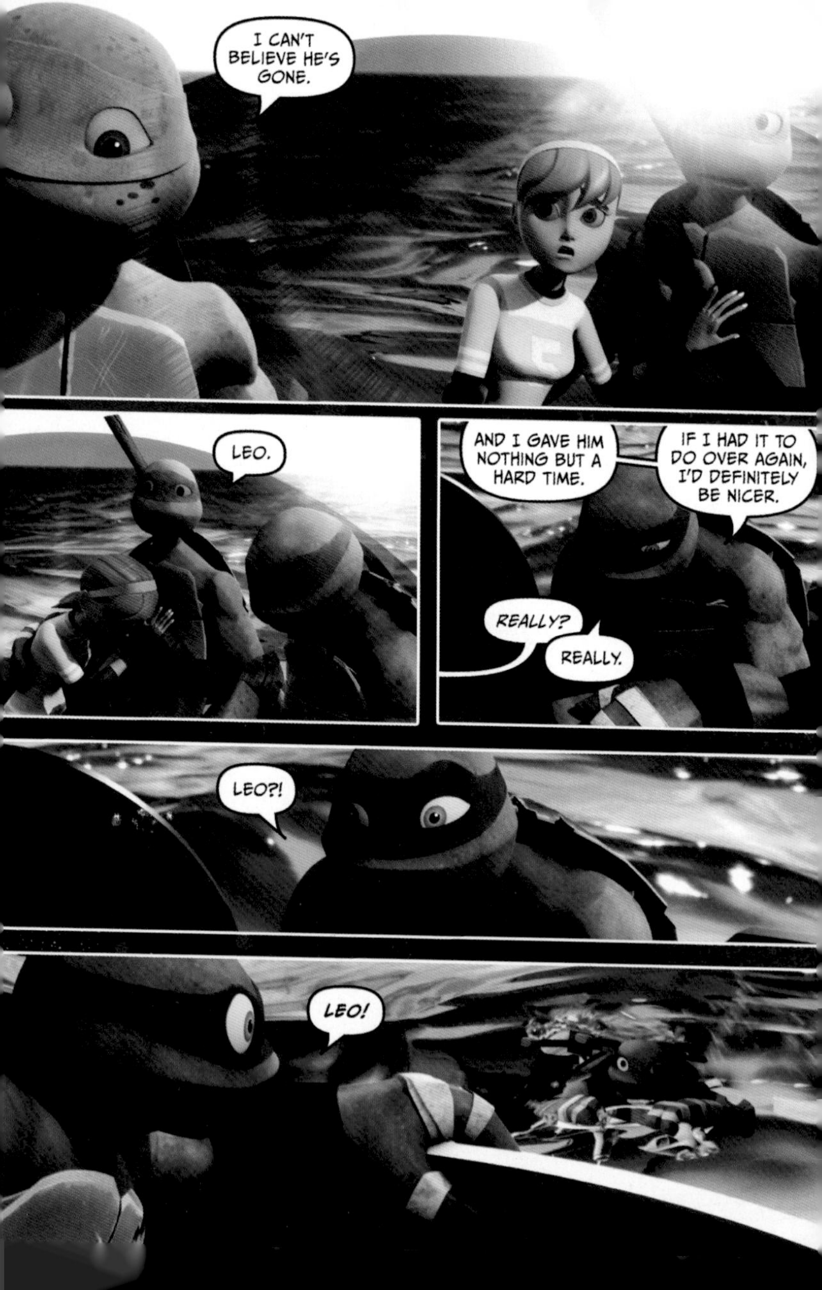
I CAN'T BELIEVE HE'S GONE.
LEO.
AND I GAVE HIM NOTHING BUT A HARD TIME.
IF I HAD IT TO DO OVER AGAIN, I'D DEFINITELY BE NICER.
REALLY?
REALLY.
LEO?!
LEO!

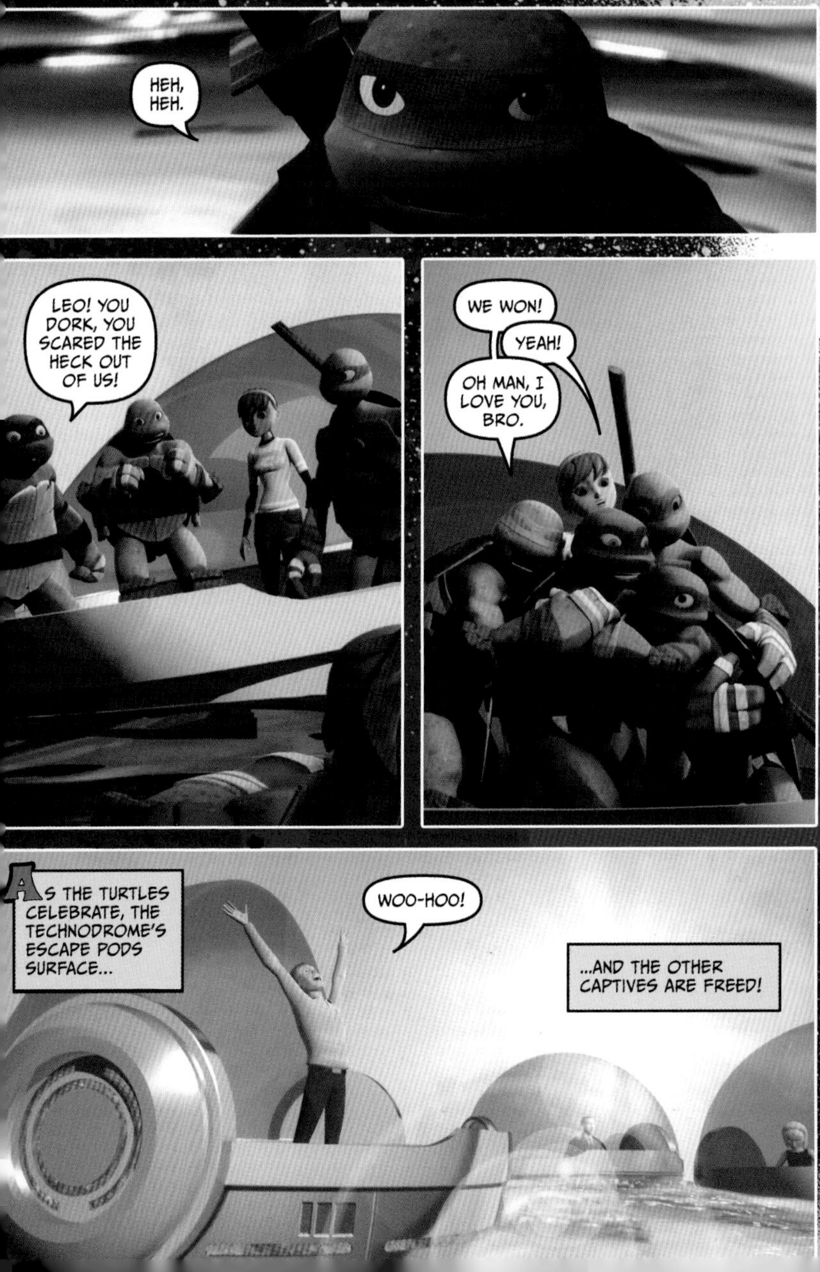
HEH, HEH.
LEO! YOU DORK, YOU SCARED THE HECK OUT OF US!
WE WON!
YEAH!
OH MAN, I LOVE YOU, BRO.
AS THE TURTLES CELEBRATE, THE TECHNODROME'S ESCAPE PODS SURFACE...
WOO-HOO!
...AND THE OTHER CAPTIVES ARE FREED!

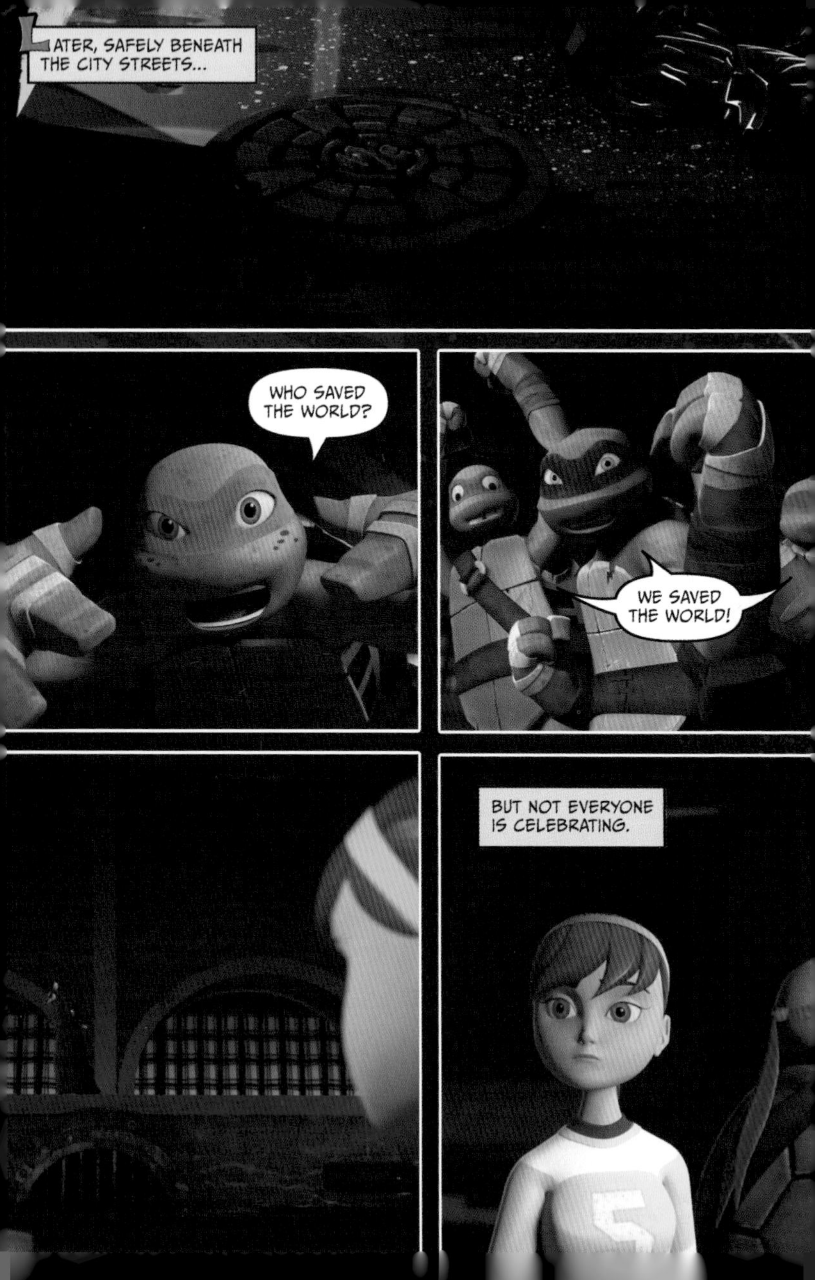
LATER, SAFELY BENEATH THE CITY STREETS...
WHO SAVED THE WORLD?
WE SAVED THE WORLD!
BUT NOT EVERYONE IS CELEBRATING.

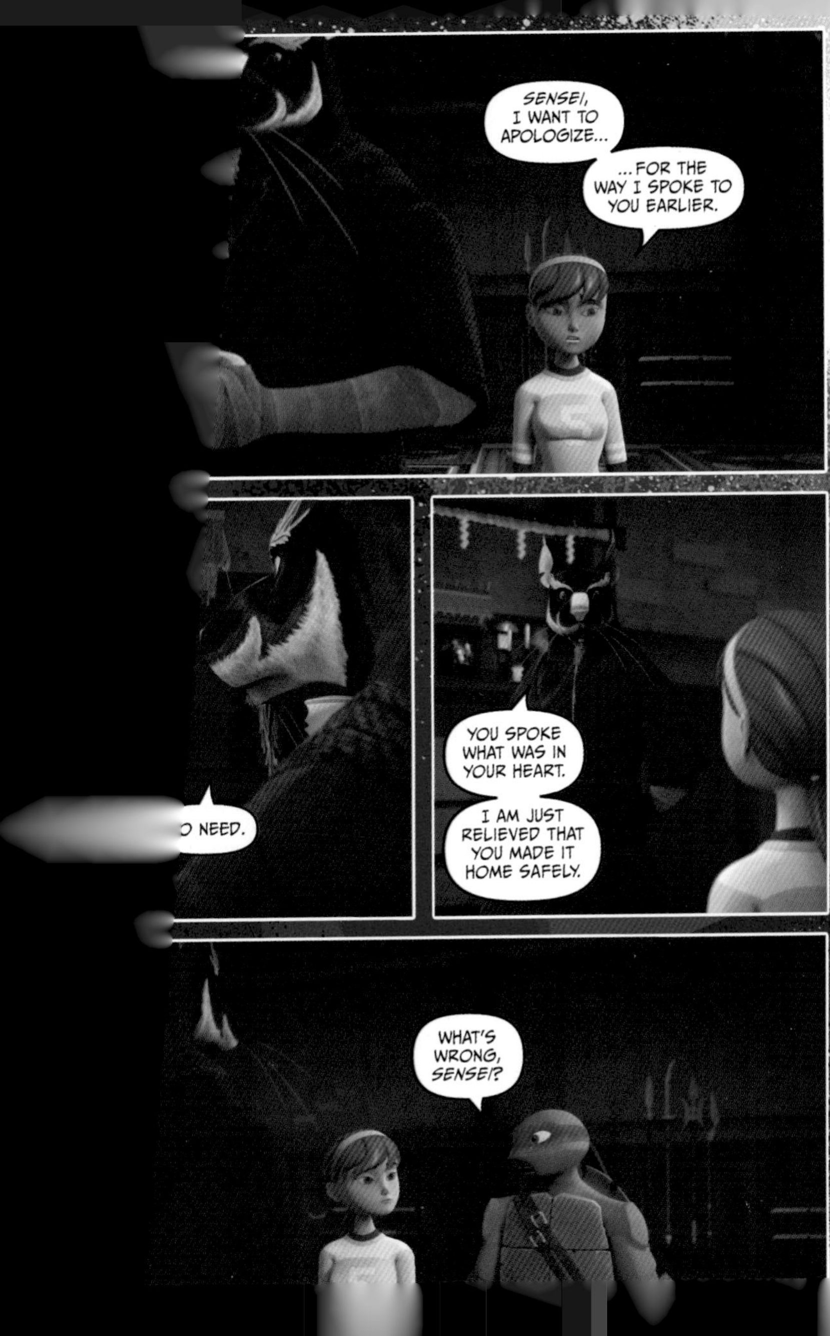
SENSEI, I WANT TO APOLOGIZE...
...FOR THE WAY I SPOKE TO YOU EARLIER.
O NEED.
YOU SPOKE WHAT WAS IN YOUR HEART.
I AM JUST RELIEVED THAT YOU MADE IT HOME SAFELY.
WHAT'S WRONG, SENSEI?

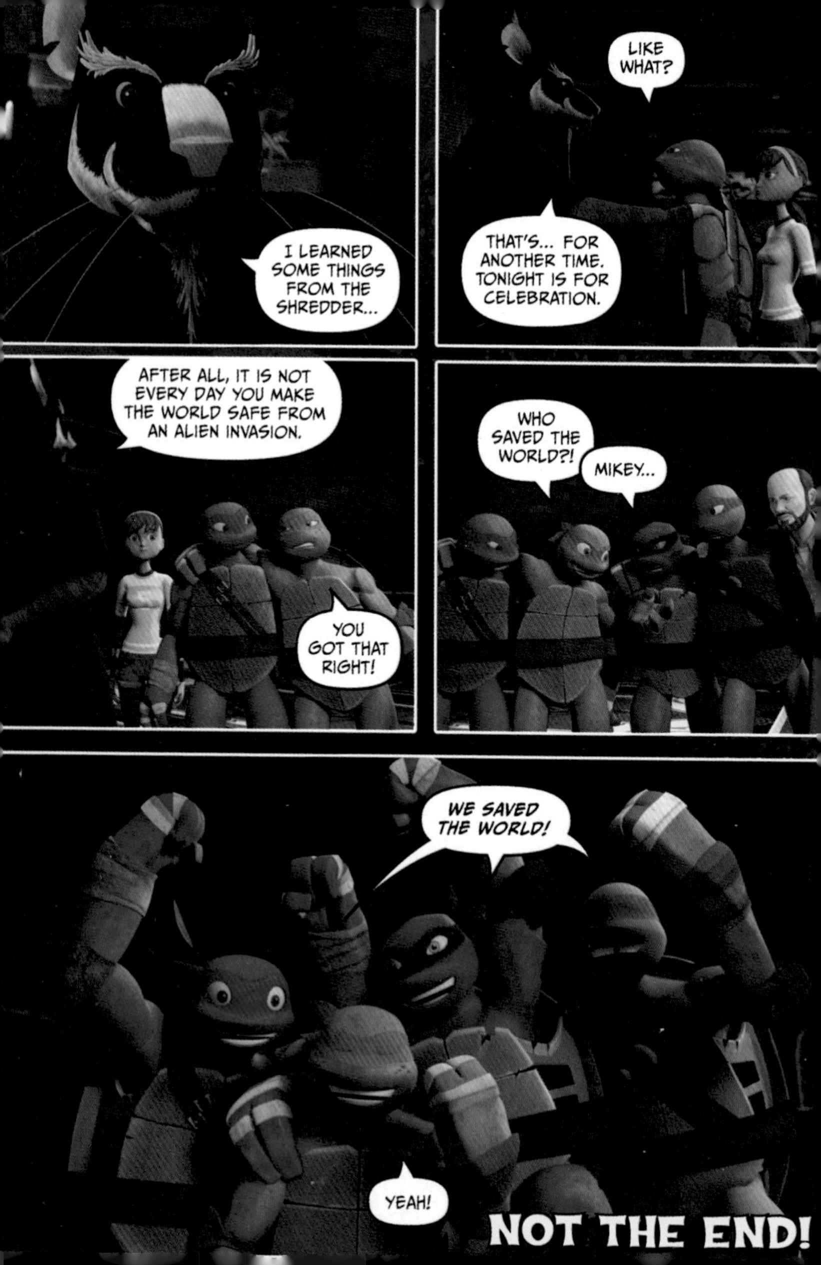
I LEARNED SOME THINGS FROM THE SHREDDER...
LIKE WHAT?
THAT'S... FOR ANOTHER TIME. TONIGHT IS FOR CELEBRATION.
AFTER ALL, IT IS NOT EVERY DAY YOU MAKE THE WORLD SAFE FROM AN ALIEN INVASION.
YOU GOT THAT RIGHT!
WHO SAVED THE WORLD?!
MIKEY...
WE SAVED THE WORLD!
YEAH!
NOT THE END!